"Low-Maintenance Relationship, Hot Sex Guaranteed, No Strings Attached. And You're Turning Me Down?"

Jack nodded in response to her question, though every cell in his body screamed, *Are you crazy?*

"You think my father offered me this job to exert some sort of influence on you?" Paris stared at him narrow-eyed for a moment, then in several brisk strides she was out the door, but not before Jack detected the hurt in her eyes.

Her pride was hurt, he suspected. Same as six years ago. Except her offer then had been hugely different. Then she'd spoken of love. She'd wanted to gift him with her innocence and that had scared the hell out of him. Now she only wanted a quick affair to cure an old infatuation.

Well, tough.

He didn't do one-night stands and he didn't need to prove what he'd suspected all along—that having Paris Grantham would be addictive and way too consuming....

Dear Reader,

Welcome to the world of Silhouette Desire, where you can indulge yourself every month with romances that can only be described as passionate, powerful and provocative!

The ever-fabulous Ann Major offers a *Cowboy Fantasy*, July's MAN OF THE MONTH. Will a fateful reunion between a Texas cowboy and his ex-flame rekindle their fiery passion? In *Cherokee*, Sheri WhiteFeather writes a compelling story about a Native American hero who, while searching for his Cherokee heritage, falls in love with a heroine who has turned away from hers.

The popular miniseries BACHELOR BATTALION by Maureen Child marches on with *His Baby!*—a marine hero returns from an assignment to discover he's a father. The tantalizing Desire miniseries FORTUNES OF TEXAS: THE LOST HEIRS continues with *The Pregnant Heiress* by Eileen Wilks, whose pregnant heroine falls in love with the investigator protecting her from a stalker.

Alexandra Sellers has written an enchanting trilogy, SONS OF THE DESERT: THE SULTANS, launching this month with *The Sultan's Heir*. A prince must watch over the secret child heir to the kingdom along with the child's beautiful mother. And don't miss Bronwyn Jameson's Desire debut—an intriguing tale involving a self-made man who's *In Bed with the Boss's Daughter*.

Treat yourself to all six of these heart-melting tales of Desire—and see inside for details on how to enter our Silhouette Makes You a Star contest.

Enjoy!

Joan Marlow Golan

Joan Marlow Golan
Senior Editor, Silhouette Desire

Please address questions and book requests to:
Silhouette Reader Service
U.S.: 3010 Walden Ave., P.O. Box 1325, Buffalo, NY 14269
Canadian: P.O. Box 609, Fort Erie, Ont. L2A 5X3

In Bed with the
Boss's Daughter
BRONWYN JAMESON

Published by Silhouette Books
America's Publisher of Contemporary Romance

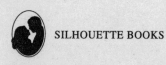

SILHOUETTE BOOKS

ISBN 0-373-76380-8

IN BED WITH THE BOSS'S DAUGHTER

Copyright © 2001 by Bronwyn Turner

This edition published by arrangement with Harlequin Books S.A.

® and TM are trademarks of Harlequin Books S.A., used under license.
Trademarks indicated with ® are registered in the United States Patent
and Trademark Office, the Canadian Trade Marks Office and in other
countries.

Visit Silhouette at www.eHarlequin.com

Printed in U.S.A.

One

He missed her entrance, but Jack knew she'd made one. She would have made one even without arriving fashionably late on her father's arm…and even if that man wasn't Kevin "K.G." Grantham, billionaire property developer and host of this shindig.

Paris Grantham made entrances because she was, quite simply, 180 centimeters of spectacular construction.

Jack rolled his tense shoulders, ran his tongue around his dry mouth and cursed the sudden scarcity of drink waiters. He scanned the crush for a white jacket or a tray held aloft but instead found her. Again. Dressed in something bronze and lacy, she shimmered like old gold against the backdrop of cocktail-party black, all long legs and sleek curves, as poised and graceful as a fashion model.

Except she would never cut it as a model. Not without kissing all those gorgeous curves goodbye.

Jack tugged at his collar to ease the stiff constriction of

his bow tie and wished for an equally simple solution to another hot, tight pressure—the one spreading south. He blessed the appearance of a waiter and snagged a drink from his tray. Maybe the champagne would cool his blood.

Yeah, right! Maybe he should just have stayed the hell away!

All Grantham executives were expected to attend all project launches, but Jack usually ignored that unwritten rule. He despised black-tie as much as he hated small talk and the absurd excuse for food they served at these things. He took a long sip of champagne and surveyed the sole reason he had come tonight over the top of his glass. Objectively. With his mind instead of his body.

The hair she used to wear loose was piled high in an elaborate style that accentuated the regal tilt of her head, the high angle of her chin, the way she looked down her nose…and how her fine, straight nose was custom-built for the purpose. A tiara wouldn't look out of place on that golden head.

Yeah, he snorted, K.G. should have set a tiara on his prodigal daughter's head and stood *her* on the spotlit dais instead of the model for Grantham's newest city-living complex. The Acacia Project wasn't the star of this show.

Jack's gaze fixed on her face, watching for some chink in that classic semibored expression favored by the born rich, something to show she'd adopted the look to fit tonight's occasion, not because she'd changed. But nothing shifted. Not a flicker of her carefully arched brows nor a waver of her glossy half smile.

And he realized the tightness in his gut had changed from heated awareness to disappointment. *No.* Disappointment came nowhere near describing this acid gnawing.

What had he expected?

Simple.

He'd expected a grown-up version of the Paris he remembered, the one whose smile filled the room, whose widely spaced smoky eyes mirrored her every emotion. The one who dared wear a tiny leather skirt to a Grantham's Christmas party, who swigged Bollinger straight from the bottle and danced like she'd swallowed the music with it.

The girl-woman who'd rocked his foundations with her clear, honest proposition and then, before he could grasp the concept of the boss's daughter all grown-up and suddenly wanting him, had run away to London to live with her mother.

He'd expected to see that Paris and to declare, without reservation, the rumors false.

But this Paris looked like the kind of woman who *would* dump her fiancé when his money ran out. She looked like the kind of woman who *would* come running home to the comforting arms of Daddy's billions.

Jack drained his glass and wished he'd swallowed something harsh like tequila to match his mood. He fought the urge to wade through the sea of dinner suits and designer dresses, to grab her by the shoulders and shake her. To remind her how he'd told her to grow up, not grow into a Grantham!

Carefully he loosened his clenched fingers from the delicate stem of crystal in his hand. What did he know about Paris Grantham, anyway? For years she'd been the gangly limbed kid hanging about the edges of her father's weekend house parties, parties that were no more than business summits in casual dress with drinks. He'd noticed her, he'd felt sorry for her, he'd encouraged her to talk to him. When she went away to boarding school, he didn't see her for two years, not until that night six years ago when she'd made her feelings for him extravagantly clear.

Feelings or intentions?

It didn't matter. At twenty-six his goal of snagging Grantham's top project-management job was so close he could taste it. At eighteen she'd been too young and too wild and too much the boss's daughter to be anything but trouble.

Six years on, she was still the boss's daughter, although everything else about her had changed. Jack unclenched his jaw and told himself the changes should please him. This woman wouldn't mess with his head at a time when he needed it clear and focused.

But pleasure was not part of the volatile cocktail of emotions curdling his gut. He recognized intense disappointment, a sense of loss and, seething through it, an irritation bordering on anger. And he knew he couldn't leave well enough alone. He had to know why she'd left so suddenly...and why she'd come back.

Paris shook her head slightly to stop her eyes crossing, not from boredom so much as sleep deprivation. If only she could summon up a dash of the anticipation that had kept her awake through most of yesterday's twenty-four-hour flight, a skerrick of the excitement that had kept her flying sky-high long after the plane touched down.

It seemed as if her head had barely touched the pillow when K.G. pulled the curtains wide on a bright October morning. Caroline, her latest wannabe-stepmother, couldn't wait to meet her. Caroline then insisted they shop and do lunch and that Paris mustn't sleep or her whole body clock would be out of whack.

At this moment she longed for "out of whack." It sounded a vast improvement over her current state of totally whacked. She needed to perk up before she nodded off on the lord mayor's shoulder. The thought of her mother's reaction to such a breach of etiquette brought a wry half smile to her mind if not her lips.

Lady Pamela definitely would not approve!

Up until now she'd done her mother proud. The Collette Dinnigan cocktail dress might be a tad revealing for her mother's taste, but she had accessorized perfectly...and the upswept hair was consummate Lady Pamela. Paris couldn't wait to shake it loose, but in the meantime it served a purpose. Its weight prompted her to hold her head high, which reminded her to keep her smile in check and to answer every welcome-home platitude with polite good grace. And whenever her smile slipped a smidgen, she restored it with a quick reminder of why she was here.

Because you will soon be part of the Grantham team.

Years after she'd given up trying to convince her father she had capabilities beyond the ornamental, K.G. had asked her to come home and help with a special project.

With her smile suitably restored, she allowed K.G. to steer her toward another group.

"Princess, I'd like you to meet..."

She exchanged greetings with Hugh and Miffy and Miranda and Bob—or was that Bill? Her weary brain whirled with names and faces and titles. Was there anyone here she hadn't met? In response, the crowd split as if cleaved in two and she found herself looking directly into a pair of deep, dark, angry eyes.

Of course, she'd known he was there, somewhere across the crowded reception room.

About one nanosecond after arriving, as though they had some Jack-Manning-sensing radar capabilities, her eyes had zeroed in on his broad shoulders, the narrow band of white collar above his jacket and the thicker band of very tanned neck. The changes had sizzled through her body—*he's cut his hair; he's wearing a suit*—before she snapped herself back to reality.

Did you think he'd go six years without a haircut? Did

you think Grantham's manager of construction projects
would turn up to a project launch in jeans and hard hat?

Now she could see he'd changed in other ways. He didn't
wink or grin crookedly or lift his glass in greeting, and she
neither recognized nor understood the fierce anger burning
in his eyes. He handed his glass to someone on his left and
started toward her with steady purpose.

Oh, help!

For all her anticipation when choosing a dress to knock
his socks off, despite her practice of witty opening lines,
she wasn't ready to face him. Not now. Not tired and fuzzy-
headed.

She turned and excused her way through the crowd, but
her skirt was too slim and her heels too high for a rapid
escape. Finally she fell out the door into the wide and re-
freshingly empty lobby, but she paused only long enough
to recall the resolve on Jack's face. Then she headed
straight for the Ladies sign. When she pushed through the
door into the anteroom, the air rushed from her lungs in a
heartfelt whoosh.

Sanctuary with a plump suede lounge setting.

She slumped into the nearest chair, took off her shoes,
propped her bare feet on the occasional-table, and closed
her eyes.

"Hiding, princess?"

Paris jolted upright. Only one person ever applied such
mocking emphasis to K.G.'s pet name for her…and he was
helping himself to the seat directly opposite. Had she really
thought a Ladies sign would give him pause?

"Not hiding, resting," she corrected. "My feet."

His gaze dropped to her feet, and she stared in horrified
fascination as his long, dark fingers circled her ankle. She
stopped breathing when his thumb traced a strap mark

across the bridge of her foot. A languorous warmth stole up her leg, past her knees, into her thighs....

"No wonder your feet hurt," he growled. "Your shoes are too tight."

Abruptly he let her go, and somehow Paris managed to slide both feet from the table. She jammed them solidly on the floor and pressed her knees together, as if that might prevent the spread of traitorous heat.

"My feet are swollen from the flight," she said archly. And it felt as if her tongue might be, too. "Which is why I'm sitting here resting them."

His eyes narrowed a fraction, but they didn't leave hers, not even for a heartbeat. "Funny. I had the impression you were running away from me."

"And why would I do that?"

He shrugged. "Beats me. Maybe running away has become a habit with you."

His mocking tone needled, but she didn't allow herself to respond. Instead she ran through her mother's checklist. Posture straight. Head up. Smile in place. Cool retort. Except she couldn't think of a cool retort. Her brain felt as foggy as a London morning.

"Nothing to say, princess? Don't you want to talk about running away?"

"I thought we'd established I was resting my feet."

"I didn't mean tonight."

Paris wished he would lean back in his chair. From this close she could feel his irritation whipping across the table and snapping at the edges of her composure. *Stay cool,* she intoned silently. Then, as if his meaning had only just gelled, she allowed her eyes to widen. "Surely you don't mean I ran away to London. I'd been thinking of going for ages."

"K.G. never mentioned it."

"I hadn't told him."

"No?" He drew the word out so long she had time to spell *skeptical.*

"I hadn't seen my mother for years. I decided to spend some time with her, to get to know her again."

"It took six years to get to know Lady Pamela?" he asked derisively.

No. It took six years to learn the benefits of hiding my emotions and looking out for my pride. She fixed Jack with a frosty look. "Actually, it took six years to take your advice and grow up."

"This is the grown-up Paris Grantham?" One corner of his mouth lifted in an almost sneer as his gaze slid down her body. It was obvious he didn't care for what he saw.

"Isn't this what you had in mind?" she asked with a defensive lift of her chin.

"No."

His bald answer shouldn't have hurt, but it did. Dashed expectations smarted at the back of her throat and eyes. *Jet lag makes one tired and emotional,* she justified as she bent to retrieve her shoes. He moved more quickly. Her shoes already dangled from his left hand.

"D'you really want to put these back on?"

Paris swallowed to ease the constriction in her throat. She seriously considered making a lunge for the shoes, but the thought of missing and landing headfirst in his lap stopped her. She took a deep breath and glared across at him. "What do you want, Jack? Why did you follow me in here?"

"To talk, princess."

"About ancient history?"

"One night of it."

"We can talk if you like, but my memory's not so good."

No way would she ever admit how much she remembered, how clearly she remembered everything about that night. His closemouthed fury when he dragged her from the table. Her feeling of smug jubilation as she snuggled in close in the back of the taxi he hired to take her home. Her heartfelt request, his horrified rejection, her humiliation. Six years and she still remembered every feeling, every word, as keenly as if it had happened yesterday.

"You remembered the bit about growing up," he said evenly. "I imagine you haven't forgotten what came before."

"I gather I made some sort of proposition, although I'd drunk too much champagne to recall what," she countered with a dismissive shrug.

"You invited me into your bed, and it was no mindless drunken proposition."

Paris's heart jolted. She hadn't expected him to pursue this, to take issue with her. As though it mattered to him.

"You said you wanted me as your first lover," he continued, his intonation slow and deliberate.

"Like you said, I needed to grow up. Don't read too much into it." While her pounding heart rushed the heat of remembered humiliation into her face, Paris gathered her pride, pushed to her feet and reached for the shoes, but he swung them out of her reach and slowly rose to face her.

"You said you loved me."

"I was young and foolish." She stepped around the table and lunged for the shoes, but he must have moved sideways, too, because they ended up toe-to-toe.

"And what are you now, princess? Old and smart?"

"What I am is grown-up and over it!"

"Are you?" When he reached out and cupped her face in one hand, she was too surprised to react. "Is this your idea of grown-up? Wearing your hair this way?" His fingers threaded into her hair and slid slowly back toward her crown. Paris gritted her teeth to stop any sound—like a groan of pleasure—escaping her mouth. Some pins gave, and a thick swathe of hair fell free, blocking half her vision.

Now she could see only half his square whisker-darkened jaw, half the nose he'd broken in a site accident and hadn't bothered having straightened, half the mouth that was too full-lipped and sensual for the blunt strength of the rest of his face.

But his beautiful mouth wasn't smiling. It was set in a grim line, and his deep-set eyes weren't the warm, molten chocolate she remembered. The laughter lines still sprayed from the corners, but he didn't look like a man who did much laughing these days. He looked like a man who worked more on the worry lines between his brows.

Paris did not want to smooth those lines away.

"Do you mind?" She wrenched free of his tormenting touch and glared at him through narrowed eyes. "Is there anything else you'd like to wreck, apart from my hairdo? My dress, maybe? It's part of the new grown-up me!"

Big mistake, Paris thought, the moment his eyes dropped to the dress.

"Oh, yes," he murmured gruffly. "This dress is extremely you."

His knuckles brushed across her neckline, and Paris felt the slight resistance as some rough skin caught in the georgette. He stroked a fingertip over the pulled thread, and Paris swallowed. He'd barely touched her, yet her breasts were tight and tingly, needy.

Needy?

What she needed was her head examined for responding to such a cynical touch. She drew herself up to her full height. "What's with you, Jack? I don't understand your attitude and, quite frankly, I'm sick of this…this…" Paris searched around but couldn't find any suitable description. "I've just flown halfway around the world, I've spent all day auditioning another bloody stepmother contender, and now—" she took a deep breath, because the last one had run out "—and now I have to put up with you glowering at me and pawing me and ruining my hair... What are you—don't you da—"

His mouth descended to hers, swallowing the rest of the word and the rest of her complaints. Not that Paris remembered what they were. They fled her brain the instant his lips closed over hers. Some dim recess registered the soft thump of her shoes hitting the carpeted floor, the rough strength of his hands on her shoulders, the brush of his unbuttoned jacket against her body, the accelerated thud of her heartbeat.

For a time she managed to concentrate on the taste of frustrated anger—and then she needed to breathe. With her nose hard up against his cheek, she inhaled the scent of his skin, discovered it hadn't changed. No fancy cologne to match the fancy suit, no conservative aftershave to match the barbershop cut, just strong elemental outdoors male. She uncurled her fingers from the tight fists crushed between their bodies and gripped his jacket, anchoring herself against a sudden weakness in her knees.

His mouth eased its rough pressure, and for the barest moment Paris savored his gentled caress, the fleeting brush of his thumbs against her neck, the fullness of his lips on hers. And then those lips retreated as suddenly as they'd advanced, leaving her swamped by conflicting emotions. Shocked confusion registered in his eyes, too, but was quickly displaced by the same old fierce-eyed irritation.

Carefully Paris released her grip on his lapels. Casually she smoothed out the creases. Deliberately she coaxed her mouth into a facsimile of a smile. "If that's a sample of what I missed out on six years ago, I can count myself lucky,'' she drawled.

His eyes glinted dangerously, and his hold on her shoulders tightened. "You want to talk samples?"

A disturbing sense of anticipation washed through Paris's body as his head ducked and his gaze lit on her lips. Her legs wobbled, and she swore that the only thing holding her up was his grip on her shoulders, a grip that felt like a curious mix of support and restraint, holding her up and him back.

But he didn't kiss her. Instead he slowly and deliberately ran his tongue across her bottom lip, before pulling back and rocking on his heels. He flashed a tight smile and declared, "Yep, tastes exactly like saccharine!"

Paris's mouth fell open, then slammed shut.

"Now why do you suppose that is? Too much time with Lady Pamela or with poor old Teddy?"

"Edward's neither poor nor old!"

"No?" He lifted one brow. "Bankrupt, but not poor. An interesting concept. Is that why you dumped him?"

Paris shook her head slowly, hoping to clear the confusion. He was mad because she'd run away six years ago? Because he didn't like her hairdo? Because she'd dumped her fiancé?

"You think I dumped him because of the bankruptcy thing?" she asked slowly. Then she almost laughed out loud at the irony.

Yes, she had dumped "poor Teddy" because of his money troubles. Because he'd wanted *her* money, her father's money, to rescue his crumbling fortune. That was the only reason he'd wanted to marry her in the first place.

If there had been any easing of the contempt on Jack's face, she might have told him all about "poor old Teddy." But his mouth held its tight line, and his eyes brimmed with contempt, so she lifted her chin and looked down her nose at him. "I could have bought Edward ten times over."

"*Your father* could have bought him ten times over."

"If you want to be pedantic." She shrugged with a nonchalance she didn't feel.

"Is that why you came home? To play the heiress?"

"I don't intend *playing* anything," Paris said, her tone as sharp as the hurt in her chest. She'd never played the heiress; she'd never played poor little rich girl; she'd never played victim nor victor. "I came home because K.G. asked me to, because he has a job for me."

Jack snorted. "Doing what?"

Paris didn't know. She hadn't allowed herself to dwell on what use she could be in her father's corporation. It was enough that he'd asked her, that he wanted her help. But she wasn't about to admit that to the man standing before her, dripping disdain. She lifted her chin. "Maybe there's a suitable job in *your* department."

Something flickered in his eyes. *Well, well, well...*

"Come to think of it, I'd rather enjoy working in your office. I shall have to speak to Daddy about it." Paris knew she sounded snooty, but she considered it fair payback for his playing-the-heiress crack.

For a long moment he stared at her, his eyes dark and unreadable. Then he turned on his heel and strode away, only pausing when Paris called after him, "I guess I'll be seeing you around, Jack. At the office."

His hand flattened against the back of the door for no more than a second before he pushed through without a backward glance or a final word, leaving Paris itching with dissatisfaction. She wanted to stalk out the door after him, to hurl something at his retreating back, even if it was only a demand that he come back and finish their argument.

Not that she had a clue how to conclude an argument that had no point.

With an exasperated sigh she turned, and when she caught sight of her disheveled image in the full-length mirror she almost laughed out loud, although the laughter would have been harsh and humorless. She looked like an illustration of how her evening had gone.

She looked a mess.

So much for all her mother's lessons in poise. So much for the slick, sophisticated image. So much for her expectations for tonight. Expectations based on adolescent dreams, she decided with a rueful shake of her head. For in her dreams Jack still had laughing eyes the color of milk chocolate and a quick grin that made her heart flip-flop and her throat squeeze tight.

Had she really expected that four years as K.G.'s right-hand man wouldn't have changed him? No. She had expected changes, and she had feared those changes…and the likelihood they would make no difference: that she would meet his eyes across the room and feel the same earth-shifting connection she'd felt at that party six years ago; that she would fall headlong in love with a man as work-focused as her father. Her worst nightmare.

She swung away from the mirror and lifted her chin. The man Jack Manning had become deserved neither her dreams nor her expectations. What he deserved was to walk into his office on Monday to find her working alongside him.

Nice fantasy, Paris.

The chances of K.G. giving her the job she requested were about on a par with her chances of finding a man who would love her for herself. Nada, zilch and zero.

Two

Jack answered his mobile phone on the first ring, then crooked it between shoulder and ear to pull on his second running shoe.

"Glad I caught you," K.G. said without preamble. "Thought you'd be in that sweatbox of a gym by now."

"I slept in."

"That'll be the day. You coming into the office this morning?"

"Briefly."

"Good." The word wasn't much more than a grunt. "My office at ten."

Jack scowled at the dead phone for a moment, then tossed it onto his bed.

No Can you fit in a meeting?

No Does ten o'clock suit you?

Jack shook his head in disgust, dragged on a sweatshirt and headed for the front door. By ten o'clock he should be midway through a meeting with Dan Lehmann, the electrical contractor on the Milson Landing Project. Rescheduling would muck up Lehmann's day, and the day was Saturday, theoretically part of the weekend. And as he jogged down the driveway he asked himself, not for the first time, why he put up with his boss's high-handedness.

The answer used to be simple. K.G. had given him all the breaks he deserved and then some. Where else could a kid who'd left school at the minimum age make it to a corner office on the eighteenth floor? Who else would put a tradesman without a fancy business degree in charge of multimillion-dollar projects?

He lived with K.G.'s peremptory attitude because the son of a b… knew the construction business like no one else, and ever since he'd taken Jack under his wing, he'd been free with that knowledge. In return he expected hard work and loyalty. Jack gave him both and then some…but not for much longer.

A matter of a few short months—less, if he was lucky— and he was gone. The leaving came two years later than he'd planned, and there would be no more K.G.-manipulated delays. It was time to get back to the blueprint for Jack Manning's life.

At the end of his long driveway he turned left onto the deserted early-morning road and set off at a steady lope. He would rather be at his "sweatbox of a gym" pounding a punching bag instead of the tarmac, but this morning he'd slept through his internal alarm. He didn't much enjoy running, but he owed his body the exercise, and he always fulfilled his obligations. He ran, and he thought about the satisfying thud of leather against leather and the even more satisfying release of frustrated energy.

Yeah, pounding a punching bag would feel real good this morning. Much more satisfying than pounding his pillow the way he'd done for the two nights since the Acacia bash, since Paris Grantham sashayed back into his life with her nose stuck in the air and her plastic smile and her cool eyes.

And her leg warming your hand through the smooth silk of her stocking, and her fingers gripping your jacket, and her lips soft and yielding under yours....

Jack swore and punched out at the crisp morning air with a left-right combination.

Why the hell had he kissed her? What had he been thinking?

Simple.

He hadn't been thinking; he'd been reacting. To deep-seated disappointment, to long-term frustration, to an intense desire to wipe that synthetic smile from her lips.

He'd reacted to the futility of a memory he could no longer brick in behind that carefully constructed retaining wall in his mind, a memory that haunted his dreams and stole his sleep. A dream-memory where she danced on a table in a tiny skirt and knee-high boots, watching him through her wild tangle of hair with eyes not steel cool but smelter hot. And while the crowd yelled encouragement, she unbuttoned her shirt, her eyes fixed on his, daring him to stop her.

He did.

He dragged her from the table and felt her body mould itself to his, soft and pliant and accepting. Dream memories of her lips, wide and smiling, against his neck. Her soft laughter, warm and sweet against his skin. Her words, her honesty, his inability to absorb it all.

He'd been pinning some kind of loopy expectations on a six-year-old memory. *What a fool!*

He jabbed at the air again, but without much conviction. After all, she was a Grantham, and the more like her parents she turned out to be—cold like her mother, manipulative like her father—the easier it would be to remember she had no place in his life.

As he topped the long uphill rise and lengthened his stride toward the intersection, he tried not to think about her parting thrust and K.G.'s early-morning phone call, or the fact that the two might be related.

He told himself the queer feeling in his gut was hunger.

K.G. wouldn't do it. Milson Landing was too big a project, its success too important to the company's bottom line to risk on a whim, even if that whim belonged to his precious only daughter.

Jack slowed to take the corner into Sycamore Road and automatically started scanning for the Ridleys' deranged fox terrier.

There was no connection between K.G.'s summons and her threat to seek out a job in Jack's office.

The foxy came out of the shrubs at the front of lot nine, but Jack dodged the open jaws with ease and sprinted out of range. The mutt didn't even get close.

He kept up a punishing pace for another two Ks, until the sweat ran freely down his back and the breath rasped harsh in his throat. Only then did he slacken off.

The uneasiness in his stomach didn't.

Three hours later it churned like a cement mixer when he caught sight of the woman crossing Grantham's car park. Not because of her long-legged stride or the skirt that drew attention to it, but because it was Paris Grantham.

Jack bent to pick up the keys he'd dropped and told his stomach not to jump to conclusions. Two people arriving at the same building at the same time didn't necessarily mean they were there for the same meeting. Could be coincidence.

On a Saturday morning, with the car park all but empty? Yeah, right!

He pocketed his keys and headed for the lift bay, where she waited in her little yellow dress, smooth bare legs and strappy high heels. But when she turned and smiled, the action was quick and not quite smooth, as if driven by nerves.

"Fancy meeting you here," she said brightly.

Jack punched the lift button and decided he'd been way off beam about the nerves. She looked too cool and polished to be nervous. His cement mixer switched to turbo.

"Princess," he greeted her evenly. "Looks like you've got the jet lag beat."

"Yes. And my feet are back to normal size."

This time her smile was real and ripe with early-summer sunshine. It took Jack a count of three to control his light-headed dizziness, and he jibbed himself about sunstroke in a dim basement. It was more likely a result of terminal tiredness. To avoid that smile, he looked down at her feet. They arched inside her sexy shoes, and the way his body reacted, she might as well have arched them right over his....

Don't even think about it, he told himself, lifting his gaze quickly. "Is there any reason why you wear those things?" he growled, annoyed with himself as much as her.

Her smile dimmed, and irritation sparked in her eyes. "They match my dress."

He noted how the dress was perfectly plain apart from the bright color and the fact that it skimmed every curve of her body and ended a good six inches above her knees. His gaze kept on sliding downward, and about halfway to her ankles he decided the legs were a perfect match for the dress, forget the shoes!

And then he remembered why she was here and why he

was here, and his eyes snapped back to hers. "Are you here to see your father?" he asked.

"Yes, as a matter of fact. He asked me to come in. It's about this job he has for me." The elevator pinged its arrival, and she ambled past him, holding the doors when he didn't follow. "Coming?"

He stepped into the lift, and she pressed the top button— K.G.'s floor. Jack swore beneath his breath. "Tell me you're working for your father."

"God, I hope not!"

Their eyes met and held, hers wide with mock horror— or maybe not so mock. No one wanted to work directly with K.G., not even his daughter. A wry smile tugged at Jack's lips, then her eyes slid down to his mouth, and as quickly as that the mood shifted.

He wondered if she was thinking about the other night, about how he'd kissed her in anger and frustration. Heat closed around him, along with the drift of her perfume, something unexpectedly soft and warm. He badly needed to loosen his tie, and usually that didn't happen for at least two hours.

Floor fifteen, he noted. Still four to go.

Why was this lift so damned slow?

He made a mental note to speak to the building manager about having it serviced. Eyes trained on the indicator, he returned to the question she'd so neatly sidestepped. "What is this job, exactly?"

"He didn't *exactly* say…"

Eighteen.

"…although he did mention a special PR project."

Nineteen.

Ping.

Jack knew, without a shadow of a doubt, which project. He'd petitioned K.G. for weeks about appointing a PR person to Milson Landing, with no response. He hadn't wanted to believe K.G. would do something this shortsighted, this foolhardy.

Taking the three steps out of the lift required enormous effort—maybe it was the weight of all that cement in his belly.

Paris flicked her hair back and started down the corridor, even though Jack was slow to follow. She wanted, so badly, to ask why he was here, what this was all about, but she didn't want to let on how little she knew. K.G. had done his don't-you-worry-your-pretty-little-head thing when she'd pressed him for details, and her hopes of earning his respect through a working relationship had plummeted.

Everything with Jack might have changed in six years, but nothing with K.G. had changed a bit.

She didn't know why he'd asked her to come home, but it wasn't because he'd suddenly recognized her true worth. The bad feeling in the pit of her stomach intensified. K.G.'s reasons involved Jack—they must, or why was he following her down the corridor? She knew he was there because the back of her neck prickled with awareness, even though the thick carpeting muted their footfalls. On this floor everything was muted, beige, restrained, as if subdued by her father's personality.

Despite it being Saturday, K.G.'s secretary sat guarding the portals of power. Evelyn inspected Paris over the top of her glasses, her eyes beetling over the yellow dress, her mouth pursing at its length. Evelyn's disapproval dated back to the day she'd caught Paris feeding papers from her father's briefcase into the shredder.

Paris's seven-year-old reasoning had been simple. If there were no papers, then her father would have no work, thus he would come to her ballet concert. Of course Evelyn hadn't understood her reasoning, and she doubted her father had, either. He'd laughed and indulgently scrubbed her hair, but he hadn't come to her concert.

Paris lifted her chin. "He's expecting us," she stated imperiously as she breezed toward K.G.'s door.

Evelyn bounded out from behind her desk and took charge of the door handle, effectively stopping any unannounced arrival.

"How about you let him know we're here, Evelyn?" Jack suggested with a lopsided grin that seemed to render the middle-aged secretary witless.

Paris took advantage of Evelyn's distracted state to push past.

"Good morning, princess."

K.G. came out from behind his desk, and as she offered her cheek for the obligatory kiss, Paris wished her father wouldn't call her princess in that indulgent tone. She opened her mouth to tell him so, but he was busy shaking Jack's hand and ushering him to the conference area at the side of his office. Paris shut her mouth and helped herself to a seat.

"I won't be here long enough to sit," Jack said. "I'm due down at the Landing." He might as well have said, get to the point; that was what he meant.

"Good. You can take Paris with you. Show her round."

Jack's lips tightened, but he didn't even glance her way. "No," he said evenly. "I can't do that."

"Why not?"

A moment's pause. "She's not dressed appropriately."

What? Paris blinked and sat up straight. She started to object, but K.G. laughed over top of her. "One thing you'll learn about my daughter is she never dresses appropriately."

Paris narrowed her eyes, lifted her chin and wished she'd

worn her red slip-dress. Now *that* little number reeked of inappropriate!

"I don't intend learning *anything* about your daughter."

Jack's dismissive tone set her blood to slow simmer, but K.G. slapped his thigh, obviously highly entertained. "No? I distinctly remember you asking me to find you a PR rep for the Landing."

"I need an experienced PR person."

"Lucky for you my daughter's been doing public relations work in London."

"Really?"

Paris's simmering blood turned cold with K.G.'s announcement, then surged with indignation at Jack's reply. PR wasn't quite what she'd been doing in London, but with Jack looking at her like she was incapable of spelling PR, let alone doing it, it was close enough. She looked coldly down her nose at him. "Is that so hard to believe?"

One eyebrow rose to a leery angle. "Who were you working for, princess?"

"I worked in my mother's business."

"That being?"

"My mother does parties," she replied archly.

The eyebrow rose higher. "Drinks for a few close friends?"

"A few *hundred*. We put together corporate functions and product launches, fashion parades and charity balls—"

"And I'm sure you did them very well," Jack cut in. He turned back to K.G. "I don't need a party planner. I need someone with media savvy."

Paris's indignation morphed into anger. She was sick of being treated like she wasn't in the room. She leaned forward and speared Jack with a steely eyed gaze. "Unless you've been living on another planet, you should know I've been media savvy since birth." She shifted focus to her father and smiled sweetly. "Which magazine had exclusive rights to my christening, Daddy? *Southern Society,* I think." She switched back to Jack and dropped the smile. "I'm on Christmas-card terms with every society columnist in Sydney and London—and half their editors—and while I suspect titillating snippets of gossip isn't your job's focus, I'm sure my contact network could stretch to find the odd serious journalist."

The room was silent for a count of four before K.G. rubbed his hands together and announced to the room in general, "That's settled then. Perfect."

"Perfect...how?" Jack's delivery was dangerously slow.

"I trust you to look after her, keep her out of trouble."

Paris swore she heard Jack's jaw click into inflexible mode. "I don't have time to baby-sit your daughter."

"Rubbish," K.G. boomed. "Lew needs more responsibility. Start delegating. Besides, you'll fit in with Jack's schedule, won't you, princess?"

Baby-sit? Fit in with *his* schedule?

She exploded out of her chair and fixed on the first thing that came into focus out of her apoplectic blur. "My name isn't princess, it's Paris. I don't know why you didn't choose something easy like Jane or Kate, but you chose Paris. Please use it!"

K.G. roared with laughter. "Well said, princess."

She felt like screaming with frustration, but it would do no good. For twenty-four years her father had indulged her, but he'd never listened to her. Why would he start now?

He pushed to his feet and slapped Jack on the back. "I'll leave you two to sort out the details."

"Hang on a minute." Jack looked as stunned as Paris felt. "Nothing's settled. You can't leave this—"

"Have to," K.G. said, checking his watch. "Caroline's picking me up. We have a flight to catch."

"Where are you going?" Paris couldn't believe he intended walking out with nothing settled.

"The Coast. I've meetings on the new casino project all next week, but we might stay on, take a break. Head farther north if we feel like it."

"You're taking a holiday?" Paris couldn't have been more surprised if he'd said he was taking an acid bath.

"Have to take one now or I mightn't get another chance." He glared at Jack. "Can't trust just anyone to look after this place, you know."

Paris didn't know. She had no idea what the little side play was about, although it obviously meant something to Jack. His eyes narrowed, as if with sudden comprehension. "Is that what this is all about? Some form of punishment?"

K.G. rubbed his jaw. "You consider looking after my daughter a punishment? Shame on you, Jack."

Both K.G.'s parting words and the echo of his self-satisfied laughter after the door closed behind him convinced Jack he'd called it right. This *was* some sort of payback for his impending departure and the latest sign of K.G.'s refusal to accept his resignation in good grace.

First he'd delayed Jack's departure by offering him sole management of the Landing Project...if he saw it through to completion. Then he insisted on keeping the pending resignation a secret until he'd decided on a successor, a move he still hadn't made. Jack had concurred, because although Grantham's good word might not make a lick of difference to the success of his new business venture, his bad word could destroy it.

For the same reason, he now found himself saddled with the last person he wanted alongside him as the most important project of his career reached its culmination.

He had to accept it, but he didn't have to like it.

His right hand fashioned a fist, but he didn't punch the

door that had closed in K.G.'s wake. He squeezed tight around his frustration, containing it within that fisted hand. Then he turned to face her.

"You asked him to give you this job, didn't you?"

She gave a perplexed little shrug. "How could I ask for a job I didn't know existed?"

"Come off it, Paris! You asked your father for a job in my office because of the other night, and K.G. didn't even stop to consider whether you're suitable or not."

"What makes you so sure I'm unsuitable?" she asked, and there was something about the way she looked at him, all high and mighty, that really riled Jack. That and the way she totally ignored his mention of the other night. "If you like, I can supply you with a list of my credentials."

"One, your surname's Grantham. Two, you have contacts in some dubious sections of the media. Not much of a list."

Her eyes flared with the impact of his direct hit, but she simply lifted her chin higher and spoke with cool, crisp diction. "Why don't you tell me what this job entails, and I will tell you if I can do it?"

"The question isn't whether you can do the work but if you can work with my staff. Frankly, I don't think you have what it takes to be a team player."

"What does it take?" she asked with infuriating calm.

"Everyone pulls their weight. There are no servants to run errands for you. You want something done, you do it yourself. We don't work nine-to-five, we work whatever it takes to get the job done, and I mean done. No half measures."

"I don't have any problem with that." She smiled.

Jack snorted. "You have no idea. You won't last a week."

"Why, Jack," she drawled, "that sounds like a challenge."

"No. It's the simple truth."

She raised one brow. "Based on which facts?"

"The fact that you're twenty-four years old and still living out of your father's pocket."

That stung. He could see it in her eyes, in the infinitesimal lift of her chin and the sudden tightness of her smile. "In my bag is the key to the apartment I'm moving into this afternoon. I won't be living in anyone's pocket, especially once I receive my first paycheck. When will that be, Jack?"

He recited the payroll procedures, because that gave him something to concentrate on other than his steadily growing irritation and the haunting trace of hurt in her eyes.

When he'd finished, she asked, "Are there any other procedures I should know about?" She shifted her weight from one foot to the other and folded her arms across her chest. Both actions drew his attention to the sunshine-bright, curve-hugging dress...and the body inside it.

"There's a dress code," he decided.

"I don't usually get complaints about my fashion sense."

"We're not talking fashion. We're talking suitability in the workplace."

She narrowed her eyes. "You want me dressed in one of those drab gray suits like Evelyn wears?"

"Sounds perfect."

"With my coloring? You must be joking!" She punctuated the remark with a dismissive little laugh, and Jack's irritation indicator shot off the clock.

"Is that the attitude you're bringing to this job?" he growled before he could stop himself.

"Hey, I was joking. Haven't you any sense of humor?"

"Not where this job is concerned," he snapped.

She took a step closer and touched him on the arm. "Lighten up, Jack. All that hostility can't be healthy."

He pulled away with what he hoped passed for indifference, though there wasn't an indifferent cell in his body. He hated how readily he responded to that one fleeting touch of her fingers, that elusive scent, the mocking smile. Her mere presence. His head steamed at her words, while his body...his body ached to eat them right off her tongue.

"This isn't hostility. This is right royal pi—" He stopped himself. Reminded himself about not letting her get under his skin and into his head. He lifted a hand and rubbed at the tension that ached in the back of his neck. "Look, I'm under a ton of pressure at the moment. I don't have time—"

"For baby-sitting," she cut in softly, and there it was again. That surprising touch of vulnerability in her eyes.

Jack forced himself to ignore it. "Damn right!" he growled.

She took one small step away, and she looked for all the world as if she'd stepped back behind that regal facade. The transformation was that quick. "Believe me, I've got the picture," she purred, all cool disdain. "Why don't you show me to the crèche and I'll see if there's anything there to keep me amused?"

Three

———

Paris had to wait until Monday before being introduced to her "crèche." For the rest of the weekend her mood alternated between near-paralyzing attacks of insecurity—*What was I thinking? I have no idea how to handle a major PR assignment!*—and restorative bouts of anger brought on by replaying any snippet from Saturday's confrontation. Terms like *baby-sit* and *dubious media contacts* still caused her eyes to cross and her blood to bubble, as did the curtness with which he dismissed her.

"I have more important places to be. I'll see you in my office Monday morning. Eight sharp," he'd said.

And here she was in the reception area outside his office, forty minutes after "eight sharp." She didn't, not for one of the fifty minutes she'd been sitting here, expect he'd forgotten her. Oh no, this was a deliberate snub...or a test. He probably hoped she would tire of waiting and leave, or behave like the spoiled princess he thought her and throw a tantrum.

She would do neither. She would calmly pick up the annual report from the coffee table, and she would use however long he made her wait to bone up on the company's latest achievements. And every time the report trembled in her hands because of the giant butterflies doing loop-the-loops in her stomach, every time she felt this overwhelming need to bolt for the door, she would close her eyes and imagine the satisfaction on Jack Manning's face when he found her gone.

No way would she grant him such easy gratification.

Her eyes *were* closed the second before a Helena Bonham Carter lookalike bounced in, regarded her with open curiosity and asked if she could help.

"I'm waiting for Jack." Paris smiled back.

"Does he know you're here?"

"Oh, I'm pretty sure he does."

The huge brown eyes regarded Paris for a moment longer, as if trying to place her, before she disappeared into Jack's office. Paris smoothed the skirt of her brand-new Armani suit and gave up trying to focus on the report. Ten minutes later the brunette reappeared. Without the inquisitive smile and wide-eyed friendliness, she didn't resemble Helena Bonham Carter at all.

A wave of comprehension washed over Paris. All wrapped up in Jack's reaction, she hadn't considered how other staff members would feel about the boss's daughter sauntering into such a plum position.

Oh, they're just going to love you, Paris. Especially when they realize how poorly qualified you are.

Her stomach hollowed as further implications sank in. Was there someone more experienced who'd been promised the job or who deserved such a promotion?

Paris glanced across at the brunette now seated behind the reception desk, studiously avoiding eye contact. She smoothed her skirt again, checked her smile hadn't frozen in the suddenly chill atmosphere and approached the desk.

"Good morning." She glanced at the name plaque. "Julie, is it? I gather Jack has told you who I am?"

"Yes. Welcome to Grantham's, Miss Grantham." Except she didn't look very welcoming. She barely glanced up from the appointment book in front of her.

"If you call me that, I'm not likely to answer."

Julie's surprised gaze skittered up, and Paris took the opportunity to smile and extend her hand across the desk. "I'm Paris."

The handshake was unavoidable but, at best, Julie's smile could only be termed polite.

"I gather you know why I'm here?"

Julie's expression frosted over. "Jack told me you have the PR job on Milson Landing. Congratulations."

Somehow Paris didn't feel as if she'd just been congratulated. "I hope you don't mind me asking, but have I taken this job from someone else?"

Before she'd finished the last words, an almost-familiar awareness warmed the back of her neck and crept down her spine. She knew, even before Julie's focus shifted to somewhere beyond her left shoulder, who had joined them.

"Having a belated conscience attack, princess?"

She turned slowly, annoyed by the little leap in her pulse and the warmth spreading through her torso. How long would it take till her body caught on that she didn't like Jack Manning anymore?

"It's not too late to step aside," he challenged.

She lifted her chin and met his hard, dark eyes. "You would like that, wouldn't you?"

He tapped the papers he held in one hand against the

palm of the other, drawing her attention to those big hands, their deep tan a stark contrast to the pale blue of his shirt cuffs. The warmth seeped deeper, looking to take purchase.

"This is an important job. It deserves to be treated accordingly, not handed out as a feel-good gift."

His curt words whipped her attention back to his disapproving face, and those warm dark places instantly turned cold and hollow. "Who did you have in mind for the position?" she asked.

"A professional consultancy."

"Then why didn't you employ one?"

His expression tightened. "I made the mistake of running it by K.G."

"I see," she replied slowly, although she didn't see at all, not without asking more questions. Had Jack discussed the job with K.G. before or after his phone call asking her to come home? Why had her father wanted her in this particular position? Had he read beyond her casual questions about Jack? Her heart thudded heavily against her ribs as she considered and rejected the implications.

No. No way.

She shook her head emphatically and looked up in time to see Jack's mouth set in an even tighter line, and she wondered what he'd read into her head-shaking. Most likely her refusal to give up the feel-good job K.G. had given her.

He slapped the papers against his palm one last time as he crossed to Julie's desk. "I've signed these. They can go out with the budgets Lew's working on." Then he turned to face Paris with Saturday's scowl firmly etched in his brow. "I gather you two have met?"

She nodded. Standing this close, the force of all that scowling energy made it difficult to concentrate on choosing words.

"Good. When Julie can spare the time, she'll show you around."

He pushed away from the desk and strode to the door, freeing her brain from the numbing influence of his proximity. It immediately cried *foul!* She couldn't allow him to walk out that door without some objection. "I'll just wait here, then, as I've been doing for the last hour."

He turned, and his eyes skimmed over her. She wondered if he'd finally noticed her suit. She lifted her chin defensively. "I took your advice."

"On?"

"The corporate uniform. The business suit." The cinnamon Armani wasn't exactly that, but it was the closest thing she would be wearing in this lifetime.

His gaze returned to her face, his expression unreadable. "If that's a business suit, why aren't you wearing a shirt under it?"

"Because I prefer a shell top. Or a silk camisole," she countered easily. "They feel *soooo* much nicer against my skin."

A flicker, barely that, registered in his eyes. *Gotcha*, Paris thought, with a satisfied little smile. But he made no comment. Just a crisp "I'll show you to your office on my way out."

Such sacrifice! Her smile faded as she followed him out the door.

Her office was on the same floor, although about as far away from Jack's suite as could be arranged. But that cynical thought evaporated when she walked through the door and took in the huge desk and executive chair, the filing cabinet and bookshelves, the telephone and facsimile machine and a computer.

There had to be some mistake. Her gaze swung back to

Jack's. "This is your office," he said, as if he understood the question in her eyes.

Your office.

His words whispered over and over in her head, setting up a sibilant fizz that bubbled along her nerve endings. With reverent fingers she stroked the highly polished surface of the mahogany desk, then plopped down in the chair when her legs started to wobble. "This is much more than I expected. Thank you."

"Don't thank me, thank your father."

Paris bit her lip rather than biting back. She didn't want another confrontation, another reminder of how little he thought of her.

"Julie is available if you have any questions or need help. She knows as much about what goes on around here as anyone. She's digging out the necessary background information on Milson Landing for you. While you're waiting, you can familiarize yourself with the computer." He gestured at the machine sitting on the other half of her L-shaped desk.

Assuming she could find the on-off switch. Paris couldn't contain her nervous laughter. "I'm afraid I don't speak the same language as computers."

He stared in silent condemnation for all of ten seconds before muttering, "Why does that not surprise me?"

Under the force of his cold glare, Paris turned her chair and pretended to inspect the computer. The look in his eyes said it all—she didn't deserve this job, and at this moment she believed him. All she had to do was open her mouth and admit it. But as she searched for the right words, she closed her eyes and placed her palms flat on the glossy desk and felt that same tingling sense of empowerment as when she'd first walked into the room.

She didn't want to go home to the empty apartment K.G.

had supplied her with, or to the meaningless life she'd done nothing to change. It didn't matter that K.G. had given her this job for reasons of his own, or that she'd taken it through sheer cussedness. She wanted to stay, to take this chance to prove herself worthy of respect—both K.G.'s and Jack's.

When she opened her eyes, he had gone.

Thirty minutes later Julie arrived to take her on the grand tour of Grantham House. Her attitude wasn't precisely unfriendly. She even smiled at Paris's first attempt to break the ice, although she clammed up again after the second attempt went awry.

How was she to know his personal assistant presided over the Jack Manning Appreciation Club?

With those limpid eyes turned killer-wolf fierce, Julie informed her that Jack worked harder than anyone in the building, was scrupulously fair and never lost his temper. By all accounts, an all-round champion boss. Paris decided it wouldn't be politic to disagree, but despite her best conciliatory efforts, Julie didn't smile again.

She remained polite as she conducted the rest of the tour, explaining such essential information as photocopier protocol and how to work the coffee machine—Paris made a mental note to locate the nearest half-decent coffee shop—but when they arrived back on floor eighteen she was quick to leave Paris to her own company…without any of the promised background information on Milson Landing.

When the files hadn't arrived by ten the next morning, Paris suspected Jack of failing to pass that instruction on. A phone call quickly put paid to her theory.

"I haven't had a chance to get to that," Julie informed her in the kind of offhand tone that indicated she wasn't likely to get to it in the next week.

"I could come and collect them, if that's any help."

"It would help if I had the files here, but some are downstairs and I'm busy at the moment. I'll let you know when they're ready for collection."

Clunk.

Paris regarded the disconnected phone with a mixture of disbelief and dismay. She hadn't expected Julie to warm to her within twenty-four hours, but neither had she expected such blatant unhelpfulness.

Her options were narrow. Two came immediately to mind, but she quickly discarded the first—as much as this office turned her on, she needed something to do in it. There were only so many ways of twiddling one's thumbs, after all. Which left option two: she needed to start helping herself. On a last second whim she turned right outside her door instead of left and headed for the elevator and Guido's, the better-than-passable coffee shop she'd found next door to Grantham House.

Armed with two lattes, she made it to the corridor outside Julie's office before second thoughts brought her to a halt. What if the other girl saw it as a bribe, a shabby attempt to buy her friendship? What if she didn't drink coffee or took it black? The only employees Paris knew were K.G.'s cronies in senior management, hardly the types you could ring and ask about a secretary's taste in beverages!

On the verge of dumping the coffee in a nearby potted plant and scampering back to the sanctuary of her own lair, Paris's hands trembled, and coffee shlooshed over the rim of each mug. The sticky warmth she felt seeping down her right leg was the last straw.

"Get over yourself!" she admonished forcefully, and with a deep breath she breezed through the door into Julie's office…and found it empty.

The anticlimax wrung a bark of laughter from deep in

her chest. "Oh, this is priceless," she muttered as she crossed the room and deposited the mugs before she spilled any more. As she reached across the desk for a tissue to wipe her hands, the vision on Julie's computer caught her attention.

"Milson Landing," she read out loud. She leaned closer for a better look at the screen.

"Can I help you?"

Paris jumped backward and sideways at once. One hand automatically flattened against her chest as if it might still the erratic leap of her heart. "You scared the life out of me," she declared unnecessarily.

But Julie's attention had been diverted to something on her desk, something that caused her eyes to widen with horror as she rushed across the room. Paris turned back just as the rich brown pool of coffee spilled over the ledge of the high reception desk and cascaded down onto the papers below. The desperate grab of Julie's hand came a second too late.

"Oh, my God...I'm so sorry!"

Julie's expression brimmed with censure. "Why is there coffee on my desk?"

Paris didn't think "Because I spilled it" was the answer Julie sought. "I brought you coffee," she supplied as a weak substitute.

The other girl stared back. "Why?"

Paris shrugged and laughed nervously. "It seemed like a good idea at the time." *Oh, why didn't I listen to those second thoughts? Before, she merely suspected my ineptness. Now I've gone and proven it.*

"I don't drink coffee at work," Julie stated coldly.

"Well, I don't blame you. The stuff in that coffee machine tastes like potting mix."

"You've tasted it?"

"Potting mix? No way," Paris grimaced. "I just assume it tastes like that instant caterer's brew."

"I meant the coffee." Julie's long-suffering look indicated she wasn't amused by Paris's attempt at lightening the moment. "I imagined you'd get your coffee sent up from Guido's." She glanced tellingly at the one mug still standing, its ornate gold logo glinting under the fluorescent light. Then, with a last coldly antagonistic glare, she pulled out her chair and sat down.

Paris's chin rose in a reflex action. She knew she'd been summarily dismissed, but she refused to slink off like a naughty child. "I didn't have the coffee sent up, I collected it myself." When the other woman didn't respond, irritation needled Paris into continuing. "I can understand why you didn't welcome me with open arms. You don't have to like me being here but, please, could you give me a fair chance to do my job?"

"The job you got through fair means?" Her tone was mild enough, but Julie's brown eyes sparked with resentment, and Paris wondered if she had a personal agenda.

"I didn't ask for this particular job, my father did. Please don't hold that against me."

A quick flush stained Julie's cheeks, but she didn't answer. Instead she started to sort through the coffee-splattered papers, fanning them out on the desk in an unspoken indictment of Paris's incompetence.

"Did *you* want this job?"

Julie's hands stilled, but her startled gaze flew to meet Paris's. "Good heavens, no. Whatever gave you that idea? I love my job." She looked down at the papers in her hand, sighed resignedly. "Jack is already working too many jobs. He needed someone to take work off his shoulders, not to add to his workload."

The same old argument, Paris thought, with an irritated

shake of her head. But then something about the heat in Julie's defense of her boss caused her thoughts to back up a step. And before she could censor those thoughts, she blurted, "Do you have something going with Jack?"

Shock, swift and immediate, widened Julie's eyes. "Good heavens, no." She blew out a disbelieving gust of breath. "I mean, he is the most wonderful boss, but there's no way we could, that I could…" She shook her head, apparently speechless.

"Because he's your boss?"

"Because he's not the least bit interested in me." She glanced at Paris, and a small glint of unexpected humor danced in her eyes. "And if he was, Warren would break every bone in his body."

"Warren?"

"My boyfriend. He's a little possessive." The look in her eyes indicated that she didn't mind Warren's possessiveness one bit.

Paris smiled back because she couldn't help herself. Her heart felt lighter—because Julie had shared something personal, not because that something had any special ramifications, she told herself.

But as quickly as they'd connected, Julie seemed to pull back. Her smile faded. "I suppose you want those Landing files. I told you I'd call when I had them together."

"And I wanted to help."

Julie looked at the papers spread before her. "I wish you hadn't."

For the first time Paris took a good look at the pages. "They're ruined, aren't they?"

"Pretty much." Julie shrugged. "They're all on computer. I can reprint them."

"Can I help?" Paris offered impulsively.

Julie considered the offer for a long moment. "I guess

you could. That would give me time to get you those files."
She peeled one letter from the desk and held it up for Paris
to see. "This reference number...here...corresponds to the
file name in my computer. They're in different directories,
but you can find them by doing a search." She looked up
and must have caught the bewildered look on Paris's face.
"You do know how to find a file, don't you?"

"I could learn."

Julie turned away. "It will be quicker if I do it myself."

This time Paris did feel like slinking away. Only the
thought of spending another day doing nothing stopped her.
"There is one other thing." Julie's expression was so put-
upon that Paris lifted her chin automatically. "I want to
arrange a meeting with the real estate agents who are marketing the Landing. Do you have their names?"

"They will be in the files."

If I ever get them. Paris suppressed the thought with
some difficulty...until she was left looking over the reception desk at the top of Julie's bent head. *Well, damn you,
Julie McClure!* "Do you want me to help lighten your
boss's workload, or was that all empty rhetoric?"

Julie lifted her head and blinked in surprise.

"Jack told me you know as much about Grantham's as
anyone, so I imagine you could find me those names without too much inconvenience."

Twenty seconds later Paris had the information she
needed, and her smile was genuine. "Thank you, Julie. And
I really am sorry about the coffee."

Julie didn't acknowledge the apology, nor did she smile
in return, and Paris returned to her own office with added
determination in her stride. She would prove them all
wrong, and she fervently hoped she would be able to do so
without asking for any help from Jack Manning's personal
assistant.

* * *

For once Paris didn't mind employing the power of her surname—it ensured that two real estate executives were available for a late lunch meeting at short notice.

And when she arrived back at her office, the requested files sat in one neat stack in the very center of her desk. As she stood just inside the door staring at them, Paris didn't feel any of the satisfaction or exhilaration she'd expected. All the while, as she slowly rounded the desk and stowed her bag, as she opened her top drawer and withdrew a notepad and pen and placed them in front of her, as she sat and straightened her skirt, she kept her eyes on the daunting stack.

It didn't shrink any.

"You asked for it, Paris Grantham. Don't complain because you've got it," she murmured as she selected the very top file and positioned it squarely in front of her. Big gold lettering pronounced Milson Landing, and Paris felt her stomach dip as the size of what she'd taken on finally registered. She swung her chair a half turn and closed her eyes.

Neither Jack nor K.G. would remember, but she'd been around at the outset when the harborside residential complex dominated conversation around her father's dinner table. Paris had paid attention because of Jack's involvement.

She remembered, vividly, the afternoon K.G. took a party of house guests across to the Landing site in his motorcruiser. While he droned on about strategic investment and potential capital gains, Jack had grabbed her by the hand and said, "Picture this, princess." She remembered the infectious enthusiasm of his voice and the deep passion in his eyes as he described his vision for a low-rise development that blended with the harbor foreshore, that reflected the water and the sky and the sun.

She remembered his vision, but mostly she remembered the passion and the enthusiasm. And she remembered how, for years afterward, she had yearned for such an intensity of feeling to be directed at her, feelings as deep and rich and big as the harbor and the midsummer Sydney sky, feelings she had wanted with such desperation she'd imagined them in the hot intensity of his eyes one December night.

Paris rolled her chair back to the desk in a rush of irritated energy. She hated the way she felt when such sentimental meanderings took over—that desperate clawing need to grab hold as something hugely important slipped beyond her reach.

Yes, well, she reminded herself, *Jack Manning didn't exactly slip beyond your reach. With cool, calm purpose he unwrapped your fingers from his arm and pushed you away.*

"And it's about time you let go of those tired old memories," she mumbled as she opened the file before her.

She was immediately distracted by the color picture sitting there. An artist's impression of Milson Landing as it would look with time, she noted, taking in the fully established gardens and the well-stocked marina. Impressive, but flat and lifeless compared to the vision Jack had drawn in her mind all those years ago.

She put the picture aside and thought about the too-big smiles and hearty reassurances of the real estate people she'd lunched with. For reasons she'd yet to discern, Jack's vision wasn't selling well.

Why else would he need a PR rep on the project?

Which brought her to the next incongruity. Why was Jack looking after PR? It didn't sound like the sort of thing the manager of construction projects should concern himself with. She released the strand of hair she'd been playing with, pushed the file to one side and reached for the phone.

Reading could wait—her research would start with a few well-placed phone calls. And while she waited for her first call to pick up, she finally acknowledged the concern that had niggled away at the back of her brain ever since she'd seen that stack of files on her desk.

All the research in the world wouldn't help when she didn't have a clue how to use it.

Four

It took a few days, but Jack did cool down enough to apply logic to the predicament K.G. had placed him in. Ignoring her wasn't the answer. Eventually she would tire of playing working girl, but that wasn't likely to happen in the short term, and short term was all he had to ensure the success of the Landing and thereby maintain his reputation beyond Grantham's.

Leaving Julie to deal with her was no better solution. For all he knew, Paris could be lording it over his assistant as only a Grantham knew how. Not that Julie had complained. She described Paris as "no trouble," and that ate at him, too, as he rode the elevator from the car park on Thursday afternoon.

Since when had Paris Grantham ever been "no trouble"?

Her kind of trouble he didn't need, not at the end of a week where problems had greeted him at every turn. Problems on top of complications, he thought as he stepped from the lift. He winced when he checked the time. Six-thirty—she would be long gone. With a trip to Brisbane scheduled tomorrow, he would have to wait until Monday to find out what kind of "no trouble" she'd been. Still, he made the long trek to the end of the corridor on the off chance she'd fallen asleep at her desk.

But she was there, head bent over a paper-strewn desk, reading and making notes. Despite her intent concentration, she noticed his arrival almost immediately and flashed a brilliant smile. "Hey," she beamed, and then she must have remembered they weren't on beaming terms, for she dimmed visibly.

As he leaned his tired frame against the doorjamb and loosened his tie, Jack's resistance was low enough to wish they *were* on beaming terms. "How's it going?" he asked.

"Fine." She swept a hand over the mess of open files. "It's taken me days to get through all these."

"There's plenty of history."

"You can say that again!"

She rolled back from the desk and stretched in one long languid motion, like a big tawny cat coming awake, and Jack was too tired to stop himself enjoying the sight. "You want to tell me what you've found out so far?"

"Where to start." Her husky laugh hitched in the middle. *Was she nervous?*

Jack pushed himself upright and came into the office. The visitor's chair overflowed with discarded files, so he propped himself on the edge of her desk, far enough away to prevent him stroking her should she do that cat stretch again, yet close enough to get a handle on her mood.

Not nerves, he decided, but scarcely subdued exhilaration.

"All right." She took a deep breath. "For starters, I wondered why this magical site was approved for residential development in the first place—not that I've got to the bottom of that one! I gather K.G. called in some favors from his good political buddies. Oh, and the environmental study was a complete crock.''

"From which file did you get that information?'' he asked dryly, and her laughter rippled across his senses.

"That information came from several long telephone calls and one very useful lunch meeting. I told you I have contacts,'' she added smugly.

"Figures.'' Jack was too busy watching the play of sunlight in her hair to let the smug bit get to him. He swore it gleamed a hundred shades of gold and amber. She cleared her throat, and his gaze returned to her softly glowing face. He could almost hear the hum of her enthusiasm. Was this the same woman whose cool detachment had gotten so far under his skin less than a week ago?

"What else?'' he asked.

She riffled through the papers on her desk until she found a swatch of press clippings. "The protests made front page in all the dailies. That *is* in the files. It's not every day you find an Oscar-winning actress and Australia's foremost playwright chained to a construction-site fence.'' She smiled broadly. "I wish I hadn't missed that.''

The clipping with a full-page color pic of the scene she'd just described lay on top of the pile. Looking at it still made his stomach twist.

"Anyway, by the time the unions lifted all their bans and construction actually started, you were two years and several million dollars behind schedule. Then costs skyrocketed when the dollar dropped. And the media's never let up on the Landing, has it? It seems like it's become fashionable to kick this project in the teeth.''

Jack nodded. She'd got it so right there was nothing to add.

"The upshot is, you need major positive publicity or Grantham's will never recoup its investment, nor, I suspect, its reputation."

"Things are hardly that grim."

"No? I'm told the villas aren't exactly flying off the shelves."

"Selling from a plan's difficult."

"Come on! This is *the* most exclusive residential project in Sydney's history. If you can't sell the Landing off plan, what *can* you sell? Besides, now that it's almost finished, the buyers can see what they're getting."

He picked up a sales brochure and flipped through its glossy pages. "Sales isn't my speciality. I believe it's now yours."

"I'm not employed as a sales rep, I'm employed to do PR," she returned.

"Same diff. You do your job, the Landing will sell itself."

He tossed the brochure back on the heap but found her quick-fire answers had more than surprised him—they'd energized him, and now his hands felt empty, restless. He picked up a letter opener and swung it pendulum-like between thumb and forefinger. He looked up to find her watching him closely, but he had time to think, *I'm not too far away—not if I really want to touch her,* before she spoke.

"There is one other thing I haven't been able to find an answer for," she said, a small frown creasing her brow.

"Only one?"

The opener swung once, twice. "I was wondering why you're in charge of PR. I mean you're a construction manager, right?"

"Correct. But I've been on this project from day one. I poured the first foundation." He dropped the opener and walked to the window, unable to sit there any longer without doing something stupid. "I promised myself I'd see it through, right to the end."

"It still means that much to you?"

"Oh, yeah." The words were soft but full of his resolve, his promise to himself, his duty to the job. "It means everything to me."

He heard the squeak of leather as she shifted in her chair.

"I can see why you weren't keen to have me on the team."

Her self-deprecating tone surprised him. He turned to find the self-doubt echoed in her eyes and in the teeth that worried her bottom lip...but only for a scant second before she covered it with the carefully composed expression he despised.

Four days ago that look would have fired him to instant anger, but today it only fired mild irritation. And intense curiosity. *Why do you do that?* He bit the question back and forced himself to concentrate on business. Her assessment of the Landing situation was accurate and insightful; she'd obviously done her homework. Her appointment might not be a total disaster after all. *Might not.* He would withhold final judgment.

"You've made a decent start," he conceded. "You've rumbled the Landing's big selling points—its location and notoriety. The name is instantly recognized, people are interested. If you use your contacts in the media it shouldn't be hard to get mileage."

She ducked her head slightly. "I do have some thoughts on publicity, but it was your idea to appoint a PR rep. This is your project, and I would like your input." She took a deep breath, then lifted her chin. "Will you help?" she asked, in such a rush that Jack didn't immediately understand.

Then he noticed the soft and honest appeal in her smoky eyes, and he understood not only her words but how much pride it had cost her to admit she needed help, especially from him. The realization that he wanted to help her, too much, steadied any impulsive answer.

"I'll consider it," he replied carefully as he decided what else needed to be said. "If you consider that our working relationship starts here and now, this afternoon."

She understood his meaning immediately; he saw it in the slight widening of her eyes and the way her gaze slid to his mouth. And when she responded, he could tell she'd selected her words with as much care as he'd chosen his. "If you can forget how I came on to you all those years ago, then I can forget the other night and the…kiss thing."

Forget? Suddenly all he could think about was having another shot at "the kiss thing." A real kiss, where he allowed himself to sink into the sweetness of her mouth, where he didn't deny himself the opportunity to touch her, to pull her close against the length of his body….

"Do we have a deal?" she asked hesitantly.

Jack hauled himself out of his heated reverie and shoved his hands deep in his pockets. "I said I'll consider it. Let's leave it at that."

She wasn't going to leave it; Jack could tell by the small pucker between her brows. He found himself staring at it, liking the fact that she'd forgotten to hide it.

She cleared her throat. "On Saturday you said you were under pressure. Did you mean with the Landing? Do you have a deadline?"

"Oh, yeah." The day he cleared his desk constituted his deadline, and he aimed to have all remaining problems ironed out beforehand. And if he wanted to keep sweet with K.G.—which he did—he had to keep quiet about his plans in the meantime.

"And I imagine my job is a crucial part of you meeting this deadline?"

"Crucial." The biggest remaining problem was the number of unsold units.

"Then it makes sense if we work together. I don't mean together-all-the-time together, I mean *communicating* together, so I know your requirements and you know what I'm up to."

He wished she didn't make so much sense. He wished she didn't look so earnest sitting there watching him, almost certainly holding her breath, and definitely forgetting the ice princess impersonation. He reminded himself of all the reasons why he needed to avoid together-in-any-way with this woman.

She's a Grantham and therefore a born manipulator.

She's used to getting everything she wants.

He didn't think he could keep his hands off her.

He had no time to think about getting his hands on her.

But then he caught another glimpse of that vulnerability in her eyes, and something crumbled inside him. He told himself it was his own inflexibility, or the irrational anger he'd been carrying like a dead weight this last week. This wasn't capitulation, this was a sound business decision, he told himself. If she failed, he failed with her. If he helped her make a success of this assignment, it would reflect on him.

"We can try to work together," he found himself saying, and her sunshine smile chased the doubt from her eyes and from Jack's mind. He grinned back, and their eyes met and held. He felt the tug of an old recognition and the click of a new awareness, then she scooted forward in her chair and held out her hand.

"Together," she stated resolutely.

For several seconds he stared at her extended hand before

he took it in his and shook to their new accord. A handshake equals business, he reminded himself, as her soft fingers clung momentarily to his. Business means no more touching, he recanted, shoving his still-tingling hand back in his pocket.

Abruptly he pushed away from the windowsill. He needed to get away before he did something really stupid. Like kissing her again. "We'll start Monday. My office at seven," he said on his way out the door.

Twenty strides down the corridor he realized how like K.G. those parting words sounded. He retraced his steps to her doorway and stood there rocking on the balls of his feet while he rephrased them. "Would seven Monday morning suit you? I have a full day, and I'd prefer not to have to put anyone out by rescheduling."

She blinked a couple of times, and Jack noticed how she hadn't moved since he left. She'd been sitting there staring into the doorway when he reappeared.

"Seven?" he prompted.

"All right," she breathed. Then she smiled and said almost as softly, "Night, boss."

Jack rocked on his feet again and shoved his hands deeper in his pockets. "Don't work too late."

"I won't."

This time he left more slowly. He told himself his pace reflected control. He wouldn't succumb to the sensations racing through his tired body. The image of gilded sunlight on tawny hair, the tantalising slide of velvet skin against the palm of his hand, the soft warmth of her voice seeping through his body.

He'd made top management because of his ability to control situations, to work around difficulties, to use the facilities to their best advantage. Now all he had to do was control himself, to work around the remnants of an old attraction, and to use Paris Grantham's capabilities to their best advantage. She'd shown her preparedness to take the job seriously, and her research showed a shrewd mind, an ability to read the angles.

Jack continued to enumerate all the positives but, no matter how hard he tried, he couldn't erase the one major negative, the tactile reminder of her effect on his senses. Deep in his pocket he ran his fingertips across the palm of his hand and wondered how long her touch would linger.

Two weeks later Jack knew how easy and how difficult working with Paris could be. Easy because she caught on quickly; difficult because anywhere she sat proved too close. Her scent fogged his brain, her finger running slowly down a list of figures jump-started his system, her husky laughter turned him hard as steel in an instant.

Keeping things businesslike was easy when she sat all straight-backed and regal, wearing that cool polite expression like a mask. But then she would go and make things difficult by springing a surprise on him...like yesterday morning's blueberry Danish which she insisted on splitting. No harm, he'd thought, in loosening up a bit. But then she'd wrinkled her nose in distaste at the coffee he'd made.

"Too strong?"

"Instant."

Her tone indicated it might as well have been arsenic, and Jack remembered how little they had in common. Then she licked the remains of her breakfast from her fingers and he didn't much care. He reached forward with one intention—to brush away a sprinkle of icing sugar from her chin—but her lips parted in surprise, and before he knew it he was stroking her bottom lip with his thumb and remembering how it felt under his mouth.

He had told her it tasted like saccharine, but he'd lied.

It tasted as it felt now. Warm, velvet-soft, and sweeter than anything he'd ever known.

He moved closer, his knee brushed against hers, and he swore he heard the crackle of electricity. He sure as hell felt the spark of heat. It leaped to white-hot life in his veins, the culmination of every accidental touch, of each time he'd casually moved away rather than acknowledge the powerful tug of an attraction that wouldn't subside.

And when he looked into her eyes and saw the shimmer of heat in their smoky depths, he was sunk. The hand on her face fastened its grip. His thumb dipped beyond her lip, touched her moist heat, and the hunger punched him so low, so hard, it took a very long time to comprehend that something was happening outside that need.

She was trying to tell him something. Her hand on his arm tightened. She cleared her throat. "Jack. Julie is…um…she needs to see you."

More than twenty-four hours later he groaned again, remembering that if Julie hadn't been there, tapping at the door, he would likely have ended up with the boss's daughter on the desk, on the floor—he wouldn't have cared where, as long as she was beneath him.

He had to start avoiding her.

With much of the legwork done on a draft promotional plan, he could cut their daily meetings back to semiweekly. Surely he could keep his hormones under control for a couple of hours a week. He knew he could if the kind of site problems he'd been confronted with today persisted.

He rubbed at the tension in the back of his neck, and the sight of paperwork banked a foot high on his desk did nothing to elevate his mood above plain old ugly. He was still glowering at it when she came sauntering through the door. The way his whole system sat up and took notice only shortened the fuse on his temper.

Did she have to wear her skirts so short? And what was it with the way she walked, all long legs and swaying hips, so the skirt flipped about her thighs? And she had yet to take his advice and wear a shirt under her neat little jackets, next to her skin. He gripped his pen harder and dragged his eyes up. He scowled as she tucked a stray piece of hair behind her ear. By the end of the day it was always coming loose from the clip things she used to restrain it. Why the hell didn't she leave it loose so it didn't beg him to do the job for her?

And did she have to look at him like that? Like she was pleased to see him, like he wasn't sitting there scowling at her like some dyspeptic old bear. Like she'd forgotten that the last time they'd been this close he'd been a millisecond from devouring her.

"Hello. I hope I'm not disturbing you," she said.

"You're here, aren't you?"

She undulated to a stop beside his desk, and her smile faded as she inspected him more closely. "I'll take into account how tired you look and give you another chance at a civil greeting."

Jack wasn't in any mood for smart lines. He stretched his neck one way and then the other. "You needed to see me?" He imagined the look on her face included concern— and immediately trampled all over the thought.

"It can wait," she said with a small shrug.

"You're here now."

"You know how we've talked about going to see the Landing? Well, I really do need to do that. I wasn't sure if I should go by myself, or when. I wanted to check with you first."

"I'll take you."

"Would you?" She beamed at him. "Now?"

Jack expelled a long sigh. This was something he had to

do, so he might as well get it over with. He definitely wasn't doing it because he was a sucker for that particular smile, the one that made his whole office glow.

This deskload of paper wouldn't go anywhere before tomorrow. "Yeah, now." He picked up a pile of messages and shoved them in his pocket, checked he had his cell phone. "Let's go," he said.

Paris mumbled "Yes, sir," and saluted his back as she followed him out the door.

Yes, he was in a foul mood but he looked truly beat…and no wonder, given the hours he worked. He started at God knows what time—he was always at his desk when she arrived at seven—and he was back behind that same desk when she left every evening. And no matter how many times she told herself, *It's his choice. He doesn't have to work himself to death,* she couldn't shake the desire to wipe those tired lines from between his brows, to restore the laughter to his eyes.

If only he would let her close enough.

Everything had changed that afternoon he'd come to her office, all rumpled and tired but willing to listen and give her a chance. It had taken her less than five minutes to forgive him every insulting word and condemning look, and five more to rediscover her fascination for all things Jack.

The speed and the strength of her capitulation bothered her at first, made her feel shallow and fickle. She cautioned herself all over again about falling for a man so work focused. She needn't have bothered. Quite obviously he wanted to ignore the hum of attraction between them, and he had been doing a sterling job until yesterday…yesterday, when he'd touched her bottom lip and looked at her not as if he wanted to kiss her, but as if he wanted to consume her.

Oh, how she'd wanted that. Last night she'd driven herself crazy with hot fantasies of what might have happened next but for Julie interceding. As she untangled herself from her sheets and went in search of a long cold drink, she'd decided on a course of action. The very next time he looked at her with hot intention in his eyes, he was not getting away with a tersely growled "Gotta go." If she had to run him down and tackle him in the lobby of Grantham House, she would have an explanation.

She looked up to find him holding the lift doors open, and she hurried in, dipping her head to peer at him through a loosened swing of hair in case she'd telegraphed her thoughts. No. All the way to the basement he shuffled through his telephone messages, that familiar twin furrow etched between his brows. As the doors slid open, one message grabbed his attention. He checked his watch and swore softly.

"If there's a problem, we really don't have to do this now," Paris suggested as he directed her toward his vehicle.

"There's no problem," he answered briskly.

But at the first opportunity—a busy set of traffic lights—he punched a memory button on his cell phone and asked to speak to Katie. Paris pretended interest in the shop window to her left. It being an office equipment showroom, that was something of a stretch, but she didn't want to hear Jack apologising for missing Katie's party, a party already underway, she gathered from the audible half of the conversation.

An afternoon party? Paris frowned and stared harder at a display of telephones. Who would have believed they made so many different shapes and colors and sizes?

"I know, sweetheart...I'm sorry...how about I come over tomorrow?" He laughed out loud at Katie's answer, his throaty chuckle tempered with intimacy. Paris shifted uneasily in her seat.

"I love you, too. Bye."

Paris heard him put the phone down. "If there's somewhere else you need to be..." she offered again, still looking out her side window.

"Too late now."

A curious lump in her chest made it difficult to breathe. Probably guilt, she decided. It would serve her right if she choked on it, seeing as how she'd spent most of last night in all manner of hot, naked, imaginary scenarios with a man who was seeing someone else.

"What kind of party are you too late for at this hour?" she asked when she couldn't live with her curiosity any longer.

"My kind of party," he replied equably. "My niece's seventh birthday."

Paris turned her head so quickly she almost gave herself whiplash. "Oh." She waited a full block before adding, purely as a means of conversation, "I guess forgetting a birthday party pretty much disqualifies you from Uncle of the Year."

He grinned lopsidedly. "Katie's nothing if not flexible. She'll forgive me as long as I buy her Dream Princess Barbie."

Paris laughed out loud, and not just at the image of Jack shopping for a doll. She felt light-headed with relief. Katie *wasn't* his girlfriend.

Which didn't mean someone else wasn't.

Her laughter died on her lips, and she turned away, pretending interest once more in the passing streetscape.

Five

The security check at the gates to the Milson Landing compound should have been a formality, as Jack was on first-name back-slapping terms with the gateman, but the two men took their leisurely time to analyze, ad nauseam, the latest motor-racing results. Paris used the window of opportunity to shake her hair free of its constricting pins while she digested yet another facet of Jack Manning's character.

Executives in her father's firm weren't usually *blokey* blokes. They chose flashy European cars, not generic four-wheel-drives. "It suits me," he'd said when she questioned him about his choice of company car.

Eventually the two men reached an agreement on who would win the championship, and Jack gestured casually toward her side of the vehicle. "Barry, meet Paris. She's doing publicity on this place, so you're likely to be seeing her around." There was no mention of her relationship to the name emblazoned on the privacy walls surrounding the site, and she couldn't help smiling. She hadn't realized how much she would like being Paris, full stop.

Jack's door slammed shut, and he started the engine. "Someone say something funny?" he asked.

"Not even vaguely amusing."

On the way to the car park she managed to bring that silly grin under control…on the outside. But inside it continued to glow, spreading warm content through her whole body.

As soon as he'd parked the car, Paris made a beeline for the nearest of the self-contained town houses, but Jack caught up and steered her away. She looked at him quizzically.

"We're taking the scenic route," he explained.

It seemed like the long time-wasting route to an impatient Paris, especially when he slowed her down further with a hand on her elbow, stopping her to point out various landscaping features. "Terra-cotta paving will go in here, all the way down to that rockery…. There's another fountain to go in over here. We've made water a feature. Everywhere you walk in the gardens, you'll hear it…. Tennis courts over there, beyond that next garden. They'll have the same surface as at the Olympic site."

Paris's feet slowed. She could almost feel her impatience seeping through the soles of her shoes into the paved pathway. She shut her eyes and let the tranquility blanket her in its soft cocoon. She imagined the garden fully grown and fragrant with daphne and may—or whatever grew in this climate. She heard the trickling of fountains, the trill of the birds who'd already made the gardens home, and she could scarcely believe she stood such a short drive from Grantham House and the other high-rise towers of North Sydney.

Time for a reality check, she thought wryly, turning to look back the way they'd come, at where the neon-topped headquarters of electronic and telecommunications and insurance houses stretched into the sky.

"We're bringing in mature palms from the north coast to block them out," Jack said, reading her mind. Of course. No stone would be left unturned to insulate this idyllic oasis from its city surroundings. That's why it was built low-rise, why each villa stood self-contained and why each had a seven-figure price tag.

They continued at a meandering stroll along the harbor foreshore. Jack's commentary lapsed from the odd footnote to silence. With his eyes squinted against the late-afternoon sun and his dark-shadowed jaw no longer tight, he looked as relaxed as she'd seen him since her return.

"Is this what it's all about? Seeing a project all but finished and knowing it works?" she asked, avid for a slice of his thoughts.

"No," he surprised her by saying. "For me it's always been the process. Planning, helping fit the bits together, seeing it all take shape."

"Like a multimillion-dollar jigsaw puzzle?"

"I've always been into puzzles."

"I bet you loved building blocks, too."

He grinned down at her. "Lucky guess."

They had reached a point where the multitude of pathways met under a large gazebo. By mutual consent they stopped, rested their elbows on the balustrade and looked out over the harbor, where commuter ferries competed for space with yachts and pleasure craft of all shapes and sizes.

"It has just occurred to me how much I love the harbor. It's so calming." Paris tipped her head back and took a deep breath, filling her lungs with the salt-rich air. "Don't you just love that smell?" Her eyes were closed, but she felt the breeze lift her hair before gently replacing it on her shoulders. "I've always lived by the water, even when I was in London."

"With Edward?" His tone was casual, but when Paris opened her eyes she found him watching her with a stillness that wasn't quite so casual. She looked away again quickly, but not before a nervous little flutter started in her stomach.

"With Mother. She had an apartment on the river for when she was 'in town,' as opposed to 'in the country' or 'in France.' I never lived with Edward, actually. He's such a neat freak—he shuddered at the thought of letting me loose in his walk-through closet." *Too much information,* Paris thought, when she finally stopped talking. It was because of the way he watched her, with such unsettling intensity.

"And you were going to marry this neat freak?" he asked.

"I suppose." She straightened her spine, lifted her chin. It was time for some honesty—on this subject, at least. "At first I only went out with him to stop Mother nagging—it was so much easier to go with the flow. But he was charming, and so attentive, and I guess I fell in love with all that attention. I had this corny dream of children and ponies and puppies romping on his estate. I loved his estate." She paused, waiting for the familiar hurt to catch in her chest. But she felt nothing except a strange emptiness. "In the end it didn't matter, because it turned out he didn't love me, not once he understood I wouldn't finance his lifestyle. You see, Edward didn't much like earning money. He preferred spending it."

She held his gaze even while she held her breath, expecting him to make some mocking comment on how she and Edward should have been a matched pair. He didn't.

"You didn't know he was about to go down the gurgler?"

"There were a lot of things I didn't know about Edward. He wasn't much of an advertisement for his title, I'm afraid." Her hair blew across her face, but she didn't bother shifting it. She didn't want to catch any of the responses that might chase across his face. Disbelief, distaste, pity.

"That's the thing about hereditary titles. You don't have to do a thing to earn them."

His words could have mocked her princess tag as much as Edward's title, but Paris didn't care. Not when he leaned closer to brush the hair back behind her ear. His fingers lingered on the sensitive skin, and she found herself leaning into the almost-caress, wanting to prolong it, wanting to feel his rough palm cupping her cheek, drawing her nearer.

In that moment something inside seemed to expand, as if to fill the yawning emptiness. Something that had been lying there, dormant, waiting for this moment and that particular touch.

But before she could do more than think *of course,* his hand dropped away and he took a step back, as if to remove himself from the intimacy of the last few minutes. He gestured toward the closest villa. "You ready to take a look inside?"

Somehow she managed a smile. "You're the boss."

His answering grin crinkled the corners of his eyes, and instead of moving off, Paris stood staring at him like some fixated loon, until the grin faded and his lips tightened. As she finally followed him up the path, she noticed that the tension was back in his shoulders.

So much for détente!

He used a swipe card to open the front door. "This one's decorated for inspections. Not exactly your suburban open house, but available to serious lookers," he explained.

Paris nodded, then walked slowly inside. She turned a full 360 degrees before breathing an awed, "Wow!"

"Not what you expected?"

"Not even." As she executed another turn through the open-plan living space, she felt the house's serenity before she recognized the architect's clever use of light and air. The room was decorated mainly in blue, with touches of yellow reflecting the sunlight that streamed through the French doors and gable windows. She had expected trendy ultra-contemporary furniture but was pleasantly surprised to find that nothing looked remotely as if it belonged on the starship *Enterprise*.

She spread her arms wide and laughed out loud. "This is total and absolute magic. I love it. Are they all the same?"

"No. Off-plan buyers had the option to do their own decorating—most took it up. This one's mine."

Paris turned and stared at him, opened her mouth to voice her surprise, then shut it again. The Landing was his concept, his execution, in his words "it meant everything to him." Of course he would buy into it.

"I bought it as an investment." He was leaning on the wall just inside the door, hands in pockets, although the image of casual watchfulness was destroyed by the jingling of loose change in his pockets. When her gaze dropped to the demonstration of edginess, the clinking stopped abruptly. "I won't live here."

"Why ever not?" she asked. "You have got this *so* right. I would live here in a flash!" She turned and skipped up the wide slatted stairs. "What's up here?" she called back over her shoulder.

"Master bedroom," Jack rasped, but he doubted she heard. She'd already disappeared in a flurry of long legs and floating skirt. He lifted a hand to rub the back of his neck—although that wasn't the main source of the tension that gripped him—and followed more slowly. Being in a room with a bed at the same time as Paris didn't seem like such a great idea. That was what his head told him. His body had other ideas, and they all converged in a heated rush when he stepped into the room and saw her look from the bed to him and away again.

Two strides, less than two seconds, and he could have her exactly where his body wanted. On her back, in his bed. Filling the room all the way to the uppermost corners of the cathedral ceiling with the sounds of mutual pleasure.

Luckily his head was still a step ahead of any other part of his anatomy, and he stayed in the doorway and watched as she moved about the room. Uneasily. Obviously she'd read something in his eyes or his silence, because her quick exploration of the dressing room and ensuite lacked the unselfconscious delight that had carried her through the living area and up the stairs.

"Want to see the kitchen?" The words came out so harshly that Jack expected them to crack the brittle tension in the air. They didn't.

"Why not?" she replied with a stiff little shrug, and he followed her downstairs.

In the cold, stainless steel and marble, *bed-free* kitchen, Jack felt an immediate easing in the atmosphere. Thank you, God. He propped himself against the island while she inspected the cupboards. "Do you approve of the design?" he asked.

"I think so." She flashed a rueful smile as she closed the pantry door. "The kitchen is not my natural habitat."

"Why does that not surprise me?" he murmured and she wrinkled her nose at him. Cute. And the good-humored teasing was good. Maybe there was hope of salvaging the afternoon.

She came toward him, trailing a hand along the marble. "I know women who'd kill for this layout."

"But you're not one of them."

She smiled and lifted a hand to push her hair back from her face, just as he'd done earlier. His fingertips recalled the feel of her skin, soft and warm and inviting. The tension grabbed him again, hard.

Paris noted it in his deep-set eyes, in the furrows etched between his brows and the familiar weariness in the hand he lifted to rub at his neck. "You really need to loosen up," she said with gentle concern. "Do you ever treat yourself to a massage?"

"Not lately. Haven't had the time."

Paris smiled and shook her head. "Wrong answer. You're supposed to say, 'Are you offering?' to which I reply, 'I would if I had some oils or lotion.'"

She'd intended levity but missed the mark by about ten miles. The easy atmosphere disappeared, swamped by a wave of edgy awareness. His dark eyes burned with questions she dared him to ask, questions about oils and lotion and hands on warm naked skin, while her heart burned with longing to offer whatever he asked. To do whatever she could to ease the tension etched on his brow, to bring—

"Seen enough?" he asked curtly.

She sighed, releasing a whole load of backed-up breath and unfulfilled longings. "I suppose that's enough for now."

She watched as he unrolled his sleeves and fastened the cuffs, then yanked his tie back into position. *Almost* into position.

"Here, let me fix that." She stepped in close to inspect the damage.

"There's no need," he said stiffly.

Paris arched her brows. "Forgive me for disagreeing."

With quick fingers she unraveled the knot before he could object.

"Do you know what you're doing?"

"This is one of the few useful things I can do well," she replied ruefully.

"That's being a bit hard on yourself."

The softened velvet tone of his words curled a lazy path to the pit of her stomach, and she needed to draw a long restorative breath. His scent curled her toes.

Outdoors. Man. Jack. Yum.

The fine tremor in her limbs caused her to fumble as she slid the knot into place, and her hands overshot the mark. In the sudden stillness she swore she heard the rasp of her knuckles against the whiskery underline of his jaw.

"Slippery material," she managed to explain. Her voice sounded thick and distant, as if distorted by the heat fog that seemed to have enfolded them. She knew she should step back, but her legs wouldn't cooperate. And she couldn't stop staring at his face, so close she could count each dark emergent whisker, so near she could trace the crinkles fanning from the corners of his eyes.

"Don't," he growled.

"Don't what?"

His eyes were unfathomably dark. Unreadable. "Don't look at me like that. Whatever this thing is between us—"

"This thing?"

"This...attraction."

Paris exhaled in a long rush and finally looked away, too giddy to think straight. *He was attracted to her. He had admitted it.* Attraction was a light-year removed from the feelings hammering away in her chest, yet she knew he wouldn't want to know about those. She wasn't sure *she* wanted to know about those. Attraction seemed like a nice safe place to start. With a concerted effort, she managed to gather some poise and to speak with relative calm. "I wondered if it was only me."

He exhaled sharply. "Hardly."

"Well, that *is* a relief. I had this crazy notion that this would be the same as six years ago. Me, all wrapped up in a one-sided infatuation—"

"Infatuation?"

She stared at him, unsure what he was questioning, hoping it was her feelings of six years ago, because she didn't think he would care to learn her current state of the heart. "Surely you picked up how I felt, all those times you found me tagging along after you?"

His silence was answer enough.

"You didn't know," she murmured. And she'd thought herself so obvious. "Oh, Jack, I developed a king-size crush on you the first time K.G. brought you home."

She waited for her words to hit home, for him to do something—*anything*—other than stare at her with that shuttered expression. "Did this old…infatuation…have anything to do with you coming home?"

It sounded like a trick question. Paris wished she knew which answer he wanted. She lifted her chin, played it cool. "Yes and no. After I broke up with Edward, I was talking to my father, and your name came up. I started thinking about you again. A lot. And then he rang and offered me this job—"

"You came home for *this* job?"

"I came home because my father asked me to. It's the first time he's ever asked me to do anything for him."

"What, exactly, did he ask you to do?" he asked slowly. "What *is* your job?"

What was going on in his brain? Paris shook her head, genuinely puzzled and now genuinely irritated with his interrogation. "You know what my job is! Can't you forget about that while we decide what to do about this thing between us?''

''We're not doing anything about it,'' he announced, with a heavy note of finality. He checked his watch, frowned, looked toward the door.

Paris bristled. She folded her arms across her chest and lifted her chin. ''Why not?''

''You need a reason?''

''Yes, I do. You wanted to kiss me the other day—you would have kissed me but for Julie.''

''Talking about it doesn't change a thing,'' he snapped.

''I don't want to talk about it. I want to *do* something about it.''

He stared back at her. A muscle worked in his jaw. ''What is it you want to do, Paris?'' he asked finally, his voice as deep and dark and mesmerizing as those eyes.

Oh, help. It had all come down to this. A second chance for her to put her heart and her pride out there for him to trample all over.

Or maybe not.

Last time he hadn't been interested in words of love. This time she would play it cool, sophisticated, grown-up. She would offer only what he might be prepared to accept.

''I want that kiss,'' she said simply. ''I want to see where it leads.''

Jack didn't need a road map. Straight to bed was the only place that would lead. He bit down so hard on an erotic image of two bodies rolling, legs entwined, between peach-coloured satin, that he heard his molars click together. ''I don't have time to be led anywhere.''

''How much time do you think would be involved?'' she asked, her tone all cool derision but her eyes sparking with temper and something else he didn't care to identify. ''The kiss might be a fizzer. Or we might end up in bed, and that might be a fizzer!''

Jack closed his eyes briefly. She had no idea, none whatsoever. ''Save it, Paris. It's not going to happen.'' He shoved his hands in his pockets, located his car keys. ''It's time we were gone.''

She didn't follow when he walked away. He turned in the doorway and found her ready to fire one last salvo.

''Just so we understand each other perfectly. I am offering you a zero maintenance relationship, a chance at hot sex, no strings attached. And you are turning me down?''

Every cell in his body screamed, *Are you crazy?* Every cell but for a few rational ones in his brain. Thank God for those suckers, the ones insisting he focus on the *no strings* clause. ''You think if I jump into bed with the daughter of a control-freak boss, a daughter who miraculously finds herself working with me at a most opportune time, there'll be no strings attached?''

Jack watched her digest his question word by word. He knew the exact moment she caught on. The understanding flickered in her eyes, but she shook her head as if to dismiss it. She laughed shortly, a sharp burst of disbelief. ''You think my father brought me home, offered me this job, to exert some sort of influence on you? Get real, Jack!'' She laughed again, and the sound grated all over Jack's nerves.

''You tell me why, princess. K.G. does nothing without a reason.''

She stared at him narrow-eyed for a moment but rejected whatever she was thinking with a careless shrug of one shoulder. ''His reasons are always to do with business, so I wouldn't know. Why don't you ask *him?*''

In several brisk strides she was past him and out the door, but not before Jack detected the hurt in her eyes. It punched him center chest, nailing him to the spot. Damn.

He didn't need to feel sorry for her. He didn't need to feel anything for her...anything besides resentment at her part in her father's manipulations and anger because she wanted to use him, too.

For sex, damn it.

As he strode to the car, he deliberately allowed the resentment and anger to bubble furiously through his system, to infiltrate even that deep place that still felt punch drunk and off balance. The part that remembered the hurt in her eyes and responded instinctively. By the time he'd hauled open his door and kicked the engine to life, his anger steamed with a life of its own. A sideways glance at the woman sitting so tall and proud beside him, her expression carefully composed as she stared straight ahead, convinced him he'd misjudged the wounded look in her eyes.

Hurt pride, he declared, because he'd knocked her back. Same as six years ago, except the offer was hugely different. Then she'd spoken of love. She'd wanted to gift him with her innocence, and that had scared the hell out of him. Now she only wanted a quick lay to cure an old infatuation. *Well, tough.*

He didn't do one-night stands, and he didn't need to prove what he'd suspected all along—that having Paris Grantham would be addictive, all consuming.

Falling in love came much later in the Jack Manning plan, after he'd established his own business, when he had time to devote to a relationship. To do it right. The woman he loved wouldn't be short-changed by the demands of his work. And when he did fall in love, it wouldn't be with a woman who fell in love with a man's estate and the fact that he paid her plenty of attention. Definitely not a Paris Grantham. No way. He eased his grip on the wheel and chanced a glance her way. So poised, so cool, so not-the-woman-for-him.

A succession of images rolled through his head, images he'd unconsciously collected during these last weeks. The little squint she developed as she struggled with the database program. The tip of her tongue peeping from the corner of her mouth when she concentrated on adding budget figures. The delighted smile in her eyes as she twirled around his living room.

He slapped the palm of one hand against the steering wheel. "Why do you do that?" The question exploded from his mouth, and when Paris jumped in her seat, Jack felt a vindictive satisfaction. She was as edgy as he was, just better at hiding it. "Why do you hide your feelings behind that look?"

Her lips eased into that polite little smile he hated. "Which look would that be?"

"You know exactly which look, princess. Did you learn it from your mother?"

"Yes. I did, actually." He felt her sidelong perusal, even as he watched the road. "Maybe you should enroll for a few lessons."

Jack whipped his gaze back to her. "What in hell's name for?"

"So you'd have an alternative to hide your feelings behind. Something other than anger, I mean."

"Rubbish," Jack bit out. "I don't need to hide anything. I use anger because I'm angry."

She arched her brows. "Or maybe you're just frustrated."

"What's that supposed to mean?"

Her offhand shrug really set his teeth on edge. "You can't have much of a social life."

"You know squat about my life."

"I know the hours you work, and I know you didn't use another woman as an excuse—"

"I don't need any excuse," he barked.

"If you say so." She turned to face the front and resumed her Lady Pamela impersonation.

The tires squealed their protest as he swung hard left into a side street to avoid the slow-moving traffic. He depressed the accelerator, hard, and felt the satisfying lurch of power, absorbed the control through his tight grip on the steering wheel. He didn't want to hit the brakes, to pull over to the side of the street, to grab her by the arms and shock that damned infuriating expression right off her face! He hit the brakes, but only to avoid rear-ending the courier van he'd come up hard behind.

Man, but he had to start avoiding this woman. She was driving him crazy.

Six

Given time he would come around.

How could he ignore a pull this big and fierce and hot? How could he, with Paris prepared to remind him on a daily basis?

There would be no more avoiding eye contact and pulling away from accidental touches. She'd decided to throw the restrained smiles and cool demeanor out the window with those useless hair clips. She intended to make the most of their forced proximity. She intended to wear him down.

Of course, her plan would work better if she saw him a little more regularly, she thought with a despondent sigh. In the five working days since that afternoon at the Landing, she'd managed three sightings and a grand total of 2.5 minutes in his company. So far the only thing wearing down was her patience.

And, she had to admit, her confidence.

How could he come around when The Big Issue would

never change? To Jack she would never be Paris, full stop, no strings attached. She would always be Paris Grantham, the boss's marionette daughter.

And what did she want, anyway? Did she really want a relationship with this man? *Yes.* Unfortunately.

With a heartfelt groan she swung out of her chair and crossed to the window. In his mind she had insinuated herself into his office, presumably so she could move right on to his bed. How could she convince him she'd wanted to work for Granthams for her own reasons, that she'd known nothing about the so-called ''special project'' until that morning in K.G.'s office?

Lost in gloomy introspection she wasn't looking beyond her window...not until the object of her gloomy thoughts strode into sight, then stopped and turned, as if waiting. Paris realized he'd been hailed by a redhead, who scurried across the open plaza. The woman stood on tippy-toes to kiss his cheek, her hair blazing its own fire into the midday heat.

When Jack flung his head back, Paris's gaze fastened on the white curve of his wide-open mouth, and she swore she could hear his unrestrained laughter bouncing off the walls of the canyoned streets below. Then he swung a casual arm around the woman's shoulders and they strolled out of view.

Many long raw heartbeats later, Paris found she'd pressed her face hard against the glass. She eased away and sank into her chair, shaking her head to dispel the image of easy intimacy she'd just witnessed. She shook her head harder when she identified the tight pain in her chest.

Jealousy.

She wanted to be the woman laughing with Jack. She wanted to be easy in his company instead of analyzing every facial expression, second-thinking every word and third-thinking every reaction.

She clutched the edge of her desk with both hands, but it wasn't so easy to get a grip on her whirlpooling emotions. Never had she felt any kind of possessiveness before. She hadn't cared when Edward danced with other women, even when they wound their arms around his neck and cosied up to him.

Then she'd felt oh-so-mature about her tolerance. Now she knew she just hadn't cared enough.

She did care about that woman laughing with Jack. Oh, she cared, and she burned with a volatile mix of torment and jealousy and anger. Because she cared so much and he hadn't even felt it worth his effort to tell her about this woman. He'd found it easier to blame his rebuttal of her offer on the strings of her family relationship.

She clasped the desk tighter, else she would give in and hurl something large and breakable at the wall. Breathe deeply, she told herself. Concentrate on *not* doing something irrational and violent.

After her third deep breath she felt capable of releasing the desk and making a dash for the door. She got herself out of the office as quickly as her impractical heels allowed. Incapable of sitting still, she walked until her shoes started to rub blisters on her feet.

Then she hailed a cab.

"Where to, love?"

Paris shrugged. "Do I have to choose?"

The driver muttered something about "your money" and "fruitcakes" and pulled away from the curb.

"My father's money, actually."

Twice around the block and those carelessly uttered words infiltrated her fog of self-pity. Weeks ago Jack had accused her of living out of her father's pocket and she'd been offended. She, who had waltzed into a ready-made job, accepted the keys to a company-owned apartment and helped herself to a car from K.G.'s well-stocked garage.

She hadn't done one blessed thing toward becoming Paris, full stop. She had spent half her working hours thinking up excuses to seek out Jack's company in much the same way she had as a lovestruck teenager, and much of the other half learning basic skills she should have brought to the job.

And she expected respect? She snorted with self-derision. All her life she'd allowed her father, her mother, then Edward, to dictate to her, to make decisions for her, thinking that would earn their love. It had earned her peanuts.

As the taxi idled at a busy intersection she thought about these past weeks, the rush of mastering a new skill, the satisfaction found in contributing, and knew it could be the same with any job. If she built up her confidence on this project, then she could find herself a similar position elsewhere. On her own merits. The thought made her smile. A month ago she hadn't considered she possessed any merits.

Once this Landing Project concluded, she had to move on. She *would* move on. It was time she stepped out of the passenger seat and started driving her own life.

She leaned forward and tapped the back of the cabby's protective shield.

The same security guard was manning the gates at the Landing, and he remembered Paris without any prompting. Barry walked with her a ways, cheering her mood with his laconic good humor. By the time he ambled back to his post, she was smiling and wishing she knew more people like Barry. Salt of the earth, their housekeeper used to call them.

Gosh, it was years since she'd thought about Marge and the time Paris had spent with her rowdy family. Marge called her family "ordinary," but Paris had witnessed something extraordinary during those childhood visits. She saw parents who chose to spend time with their children and enjoyed their company, who weren't afraid to openly show their affection nor to impose disciplinary restraints.

At twelve she'd been wise enough to know her parents would never change...and naive enough to believe she would one day find a man like Marge's Ted, a man with his priorities in the right place.

She had been walking with no notion of direction, yet she found herself at the same spot she'd stood with Jack a week before. When the fleeting caress of his fingers had reached inside and touched her heart.

Fool, she reminded herself, as that same heart twisted with pain. *Fool, twice over.*

She lifted her chin, swung around and took three long strides back the way she'd come before forcing herself to stop, to breathe the breeze-freshened air, to take in the magnificent view provided by her vantage point at the water's edge. She scraped her hair back from her face and inspected the widely spaced villas, the clusters of lush garden that separated them.

And above the tight pain in her chest, she felt a burgeoning sense of discovery. The tranquility of this place was truly insidious.

Tranquility etched in a world of urgency.

All week she'd dithered over ways to publicize the Landing, but to date all her attempts had been off the mark. She'd played with press releases until the words congealed in her head, but when she turned them over to the marketing gurus, they came back sounding even more superficial than when they left. No clever words, no artistic impres-

sions or glossy photographs could do justice to this state
of mind. People needed to come and experience it for themselves…and for more than a fifteen-minute whistle-stop at
the display villa.

Last Friday Jack had got it exactly right, whether by
accident or design. He had slowed the pace and eased her
into the atmosphere. He'd prepared her senses with the
most delicate foreplay before hitting her with the big cli-
max—his exquisitely designed townhouse.

Prospective clients deserved that whole sensual experience.

A party in the grounds could work…a *theme* party, she
decided with a tingling frisson of excitement. Nautical,
maybe, but casual rather than glamorous. A flotilla of boats
could deliver guests to the doorstep, wait staff would wear
yachting gear, she would decorate simply using rope and
nets and sails. The ideas sped through Paris's mind.

Who to invite?

She smiled smugly. That part was easy. Few could afford
so much as a glance at Milson Landing, but those who
could were her father's closest friends and her old school-
mates. People with money to burn, people who wanted
other people to know they had money to burn.

All she had to do was get them here.

Would they come out of curiosity? Would the prospect
of a close-up gawk at Sydney's best address be sufficient
enticement? Her brow knit in thought. Maybe she could
approach a charity, make it a fund-raiser—the Heart of
Gold committee could be interested.…

Back at Grantham House, she swept everything from her
desk to the floor, pulled a blank notepad into place with
one hand and reached for her phone with the other. Three
hours later she'd made a preliminary approach to the Heart

of Gold chairperson and roughed out a plan of attack; what she lacked was a date. She tried Jack's office—*again*—to be told by Julie—*again*—that he hadn't returned from "a lunch meeting."

Paris squeezed her eyes shut, but it didn't help. The picture of two heads, one black, one red, leaning close…

"Any idea when he'll be back from this alleged meeting?" she asked.

Julie paused long enough for Paris to drop her head and thunk her forehead against the desk. What was she thinking? This was not the way to build professional respect.

"I'm sorry, but I—"

"No, Julie," Paris interrupted. "*I'm* sorry. That comment was way out of line. I will start over." She paused to regather her thoughts. "I have this idea for a party at the Landing, and I have to talk to Jack about a date. If I don't talk to him today, I'll spend the whole weekend stalled, when I could be getting things underway."

"I'm sorry, Paris, but I will pass on your message."

"Thanks, Julie."

Twenty minutes later Paris started at the sound of a tentative knock, and she looked up to find Julie in the doorway. "You're going home, then," she said unnecessarily, eyeing the purse dangling from Julie's shoulder.

"Yes." The other girl shuffled her feet, and Paris just knew she wasn't going to like what came next. "I just dropped by to let you know that Jack's been and gone. I told him you wanted to speak to him but…well, he went straight back out again."

"Out, as in home?"

"Oh, no, he's only gone up to the gym." She tapped her fingers nervously against the doorjamb. "I suppose he's going to ring you later."

Or he mightn't consider it important enough. The dull

ache in her chest sharpened. "Does he always spend so much time out of the office?"

"And *in* the office, although lately that's been mostly at night."

Paris knew her next question bordered on prying even before she posed it, but she couldn't help herself. "Doesn't he have a life?"

Julie rolled her eyes. "Not lately, working the hours he does. He's totally driven with seeing Milson Landing through to completion, and then there's—" Julie's rush of words stopped suddenly. She flushed.

"And then there's me?" Paris guessed.

"Oh, no. That wasn't what I was going to say." Julie bit her lip and flushed even darker. "You've been no trouble."

"The coffee incident notwithstanding."

Julie smiled. "It could have been worse."

Paris raised her brows questioningly.

"You could have knocked both cups over."

Paris laughed and shook her head. "Thank you for that. I needed a laugh." But more than the laugh, she needed this small tentative sign of acceptance or approval or friendship, or whatever it was that Julie was finally granting.

"Tough day?"

"Frustrating. I've been waiting most of the afternoon for Jack to come in." She leaned back in her chair and met Julie's sympathetic gaze with a wry smile. "Patience is not my strong suit."

"He had this meeting about his father's estate. He and Tina are executors."

Paris's heart stuttered, then raced. "Tina?"

"His sister."

His sister. Paris attempted to stifle the instant flash of pure golden delight. Told herself her heart didn't matter, not when she'd determined to build some professional respect. "I really need to talk to him."

"You could always go talk to him in the gym."

Paris glanced down at her suit. "I'm hardly dressed for the gym."

"You're only going to be talking…right?"

Paris ignored the suggestive edge to Julie's smile. *Yes, she would only be talking. Business.* Her own smile was sincere as the other girl hitched her bag higher on her shoulder and made to leave. "Thanks for dropping by, Julie. I appreciate it."

"No problem."

The executive gym on the top floor of Grantham House was deserted but for the one man pounding away at an unfortunate punching bag. Paris watched the interplay of muscles and tendons across his shoulders and upper arms in silent, awestruck fascination. Obviously he used those muscles. A lot.

He must have heard her drooling, because he turned quickly, and his eyes found her with pinpoint accuracy. There was something in their dark intensity, something unguarded and as powerful as any of the punches she'd just watched him throw. The air crackled with it. Then he lifted a glove and swiped at the sweat dripping from his forehead, breaking eye contact and the strange tension of the moment.

It seemed as though he worked himself as hard in the gym as in the workplace.

The thought disturbed Paris, but she had no time to ponder why before he started toward her, removing one of his gloves with his teeth as he approached, then the other, before tossing both to the ground. The powerful sensual kick provided by his primitive actions drove all the air from her lungs. She felt the elevated thud of her pulse, the tightness in her breasts; then he was there, right before her.

And she noticed how the sweat wasn't confined to his forehead. It glistening on the smooth tan of his upper arms and higher, over his shoulders, on both sides of the straps on his muscle shirt. And as she watched, a single bead lazed down his collarbone to disappear into a smattering of chest hair that extended beyond the confines of his loose top.

Paris gulped and tried to focus on what had brought her here. Work. *The smell of his body heat.* A date for the party. *The sound of his breathing, slightly elevated by exercise.* Professional respect. She had to remember professional respect.

Finally she gathered herself enough to find her speaking voice. "I have to talk to you."

Seven

"**Y**ou want to talk *now?*" Of all the things Jack wanted to do with her—*now*—talking figured way down the list. One second after he'd felt her there, eyes caressing him with sultry heat, he knew avoiding her hadn't quelled the craziness. It had honed it to a dangerous razor-sharp edge.

"Well, I didn't come here to work out. That much is obvious."

She wore one of her pricey designer suits—as she'd pointed out, not your standard gymwear, yet it did more for Jack than any skimpy, lycra combo. Arousal tightened his skin just looking at her and speculating what she wore underneath. That sketchy description she'd given hadn't helped, nor had the glimpse of a narrow silky strap when she'd leaned over his desk one day. A three-second glimpse, yet he'd been unable to wipe the image from his mind. His fingers itched to attack that prim row of buttons, to reveal her to his eyes, his hands, his mouth.

He snatched up a weight and started a set of bicep curls. *Curl, release, three. Curl, release, four.* "I thought you wanted to talk," he bit out. *Curl, release, five.* When she didn't answer, he made the mistake of glancing up and found her attention fixed on his arm, her focus hazy, her lips softly parted.

"Hell, Paris. I told you not to look at me like that." He slammed the weight back into the rack, breathing harshly as he battled the tight, hard clutch of desire. "What is it you want to talk about? I have to be out of here in five minutes."

"Of course."

"What's that supposed to mean?" Eyes narrowed, hands on hips, he dared her to take issue. "Come on. Spit it out, princess."

She almost did; Jack saw the instant she changed her mind. The almost imperceptible shake of her head, the compressed lips as if she'd bitten down on the words. The movement of her throat as she swallowed them. She straightened, lifted her chin. "Maybe this isn't a good time."

"No?"

She took a step backward. Jack followed. It wasn't rational, it wasn't smart, but he couldn't stop himself. He ached for an argument, a release from the hot roiling restlessness that had driven him to the gym at the end of this long frustrating week. He'd hoped to pound it out of himself on the bag before he returned her call, and maybe he would have succeeded. If she hadn't shown up.

"Running away again?" he asked as she continued to backpedal. He was still one step from reaching her when she tripped. In slow motion he saw her wildly flailing arms, heard her small startled cry, felt the frantic grab of her hands as she tumbled backward over the edge of a bench…dragging him down with her.

They hit the floor hard. The dull sound of the impact throbbed in the back of Jack's head as he attempted to fill his winded lungs. Somehow he'd managed to end up on the floor side of their tangled bodies, with Paris half on top and half beside him. And despite the ringing in his ears and the elbow planted in his abdomen, he was instantly intensely aware of the leg nestled between his, and the soft weight of her breasts against his chest.

"Are you all right?" she asked breathlessly. And when she scrambled off him, both the heavy silk of her hair and her stockinged leg dragged slowly across his skin. Jack was not all right. He groaned in response to the dual-edged torture.

"I'm sorry. You took all our weight when we fell, and I'm no lightweight. Did I hurt you?"

He felt her moving beside him, heard the soft rustle of her clothing as she sat up. And then, God help him, she was touching him. Her hands skimmed across his shoulders, up his neck, over his skull. Another hoarse sound, part pleasure and part pain, tore from deep in his chest.

"I *did* hurt you!"

Constantly. I hurt constantly.

"Where?" As her fingers probed further around the back of his head, she must have leaned forward. He felt the airy brush of her jacket against his arm, the whisper of her breath on his face. He inhaled her soft scent until his senses overflowed, and then he opened his eyes and looked directly into hers. The aching concern in their wood smoke depths caused something to squeeze tight in his chest, then to unfurl slowly, as if releasing him.

"Everywhere," he replied simply. Whatever she read in his answer or his eyes caused her lips to part on a barely audible "Oh." Her expression softened as the worry dissipated, then intensified as she responded to the message he could no longer hide. He wanted her. He was sick of fighting it.

"Would you like me to kiss it better?" Her throaty purr resonated through his body, touching every spot he wanted her to kiss with liquid fire. "Here?" she whispered, feathering her lips against his chin. Then she opened her soft sweet mouth against his skin and branded him with the delicate slide of her tongue.

Oh, man, had he really been avoiding this?

Her mouth lifted, and she traced a gentle fingertip across the bump on his nose. "How did you do this?"

"I walked into a steel girder."

"Silly you." She smiled.

"Silly me," he echoed as he slid his hand under the fall of hair that curtained their faces to cup her nape, to gently but insistently pull her mouth down to his.

It was nothing like their first kiss, rough with anger and disappointment, yet her mouth seemed familiar, and so absolutely perfect under his. He couldn't describe the complexity of emotions tumbling through him as he tasted the smile still on her lips, but he knew whatever he felt transcended physical need. And as he increased his pressure on her nape, he embraced it with all his being.

Their teeth met with a soft chink, hers opened, and the tantalizing sweep of her tongue against his turned him to flame. He plunged deep, tasting her, inhaling her, and her trembling response redoubled somewhere inside him, warning him to slow down. He eased away, drew a ragged breath, but then she slid her hands inside his shirt. How could he slow down when her soft breathy exhalation sounded so much like relief, as if she'd been needing to touch him as badly as he needed to touch her? Her fingertips teased a velvet path along the ridge of his collarbone, tentatively touched each nipple, raked through his chest hair. When she pulled his shirt up and started tracing the line of hair down his abdomen he lifted off the ground. A roughly muttered curse ripped from his throat. Her eyes blazed with answering heat as she settled herself down beside him and pressed her lips hungrily into the hollow of his throat.

In one economical motion Jack rolled himself onto his side and her onto her back. His body screamed to keep going, to push that tight little skirt out of the way and roll between her legs. To bury the heavy pounding pressure of his arousal in her welcoming heat.

He drew a long harsh draft of restraint and reminded himself where they were...and who she was. Definitely not the kind of woman who would welcome his sweaty out-of-control body crushing her into a gym floor. A woman like Paris demanded a five-star seduction, with champagne and pristine sheets, and enough time to pleasure every exquisite inch of her body. And when he looked down at that body spread before him in boneless lethargy, her hair fanned around her flushed face like a golden shawl, her heavy-lidded eyes hazy with heat, he needed to remind himself again.

"You are unbelievably beautiful," he murmured. *Hell, how crass that sounded.* He wanted original words, ones he'd never used, ones she'd never heard on any man's lips. Ones not yet invented. The power of that notion stilled him but didn't stun him. He felt it settle, deep and rich. Inevitable. He'd known how it would be with her. That was the very reason he'd avoided her.

She blew out a soft shuddery breath, and he watched a strand of fine hair lift on the sigh, then settle against her cheek. He smoothed it away and allowed his fingers to savor her satin warmth, across her cheek, down the side of her throat, above her jacket.

A fine tremor rippled through her, and he pressed his palm flush against her skin, wanting to absorb the intensity of that need. Wanting to absorb her. He closed his eyes and waited for the potency of the moment to pass before he touched her again.

"It's almost killed me, wanting to see what you wear under here." He traced the vee of her neckline with one fingertip.

The corners of her mouth lifted in the smallest smile, "You only had to ask."

"I'm asking now."

With her eyes fixed on his, she slowly undid the buttons, allowing the sides of her jacket to fall away and reveal the finest, silkiest—sexiest—piece of confection he'd ever seen. The word he groaned in harsh reverence wasn't romantic or original, but he couldn't contain it any more than he could stop himself tracing a finger over the dark shadow of one nipple. Her breath hissed in, then out. Beneath the slow stroke of his finger he felt the tremor again, keener this time.

"Is this one of those...?" Hell, he couldn't remember the name.

"Camisoles," she breathed. "The French version of an undervest."

"The French version of a torture device," he muttered thickly, as he palmed the silk-cloaked fullness of one breast. Then the other. And the sight of his hands, so big and dark against the pale, delicate fabric, was the most erotic thing he'd ever seen. His head spun with the image, with the need that throbbed in his veins. For a long jaw-clenched moment he closed his eyes and battled for control.

As if from a great distance he heard her soft entreaty. ''Please, Jack.''

''Please…what?'' he asked. ''Please kiss you?'' And he did. Hungrily, on her desire-softened mouth. On the scented luxury of her perfect throat as her head lolled drunkenly to one side. On the creamy rise of her breasts above the lace-trimmed edge of her camisole.

Then he placed his mouth over one fiercely distended nipple and gently drew it and its gossamer-fine covering into his mouth, hungrily feeding on the husky sounds of pleasure and approval purring in her throat. He tugged the material free of her skirt, and at last—oh, *finally*—palmed the smooth perfection of her skin.

Her hips moved restlessly beside his, her knees lifting, spreading, encouraging. *No,* he warned himself even as his hand slid down her skirt. *Not here, not now,* he told himself as that hand smoothed up her silken thigh, as he pushed the skirt higher and… *Hell!* He should have known. Stockings. Sitting high and firm against her thighs, drawing his eyes inexorably to the smooth band of fine alabaster skin above. So soft, so warm. His fingers traced the top of each stocking, pressed into the yielding flesh of her inner thighs.

Enough, he told himself, retreating.

But she wriggled closer and moved her leg against his. The very thought of its smooth length sliding over his thigh, hooking around his hips, caused him to pulse, hot and heavy.

''No,'' he groaned.

''Yes,'' she whispered, her luminous eyes begging for more as she took his hand and pressed it against her…*there.* Her damp heat scorched him, even through her underwear. For a long aching moment he couldn't move, he couldn't breathe. He'd never felt such intense desire, such a deep aching need to take possession.

Then she moved, compulsively, pushing herself against him, seeking his deeper touch. Needing him, telling him she needed him in husky breaths of urgency. With unsteady fingers he tugged the fine barrier aside and touched her wet naked flesh. He stroked her, felt a deep shudder wrack her body. So damn responsive. He pushed her top up, drew her naked breast into his mouth, suckling hard.

Her hands fisted in the front of his shirt as if she needed something to hold on to, to save her from falling, and Jack wanted, more ferociously than he'd wanted anything at any other time, to be her anchor and her safety net. He touched her again. Once. And she came apart.

He held her close for as long as he dared, then, with a hand not quite steady, smoothed her tangled hair from her face and pressed a gentle kiss to her trembling brow. Finger by finger he prised her fierce grip free of his shirt. Her eyelids fluttered open, and she nuzzled into him, sliding her hands down his arms, demurring in a thick sexy voice, "No. I want to touch you. I want to feel you—"

"No. That's enough," Jack hissed through clenched teeth. It wasn't nearly enough, yet it was too much for a gym floor. A public gym floor.

Very classy, Manning!

He set her aside, resisted when she tried to snuggle closer. Definitely enough until he could get her into a bed...and that wasn't happening until he'd thought this through, studied the effects, considered the consequences. And he couldn't think worth squat with her wriggling half-naked beside him.

With all her perceptions—including time—shattered, Paris had no idea how long it took her to catch up. Jack really meant what he said. Not enough to her was, apparently, enough for him. Not only had he purposefully put her aside, but now he was putting her back together, pulling her clothes into place, doing up her buttons. Sitting up. Withdrawing from her scrambling hands.

What on earth?

''Is there a problem?'' she asked, not understanding, still spinning a little and curiously dissatisfied despite her release.

''There would be if anyone came by.''

Oh, my God! She scrambled to her knees, looked beyond him to the wall of glass separating the gym from the elevator bay. It was deserted, but that didn't mean someone couldn't have walked by at any time. Evelyn, for example. Or her father, who was due back from his extended Queensland holiday anytime.

So much for her professional reputation!

She attempted to straighten her jacket, smoothed down her skirt as best she could. If there was any chance of her legs holding her, she would have sprung straight to her feet. She wasn't into public exhibitionism. What had gotten into her?

Not Jack.

But only because *he* had stopped. Sure, he'd been turned on—she'd felt him thick and heavy against her hip—but what man wouldn't be? With her rolling about on the floor, ready to toss off all her clothes, touching him, begging him to touch her.

Putting his hand on her.

Mortification swept through her, and she dipped her head to hide the telltale flush. What she needed here was calm. Collection. Poise. She hoped she hadn't thrown it all out the window with the hair clips. She drew a deep breath and lifted her head.

Jack watched her steadily, looking way too calm and together, considering the circumstances. ''You're doing it again.''

"Doing what?"

He reached across and lowered her chin with one finger. "Drop the Lady Pamela act, princess. It's not you."

Paris lifted her chin instinctively. "You think I—" She stopped, because he started laughing. "Would you care to share the joke?"

"There's no joke." And he had the temerity to shuffle closer, till his crossed knees pressed against hers. Distracted by the amusement warming his eyes, and the way that made her heart thud loud and languorously against her ribs, she missed his intent. She didn't miss his kiss, hard and purposeful on her mouth.

He took advantage of her surprise to sweep his tongue languidly against hers. The giddy rush of heat remained long after he released her mouth and rested his forehead against hers.

"I have to stop kissing you in public places," he muttered ruefully.

And I have to keep up with what's going on here. She closed her eyes and tried to concentrate. He'd laughed at her.... "The joke was?"

"You can't help it, can you?" he asked consideringly.

"What?"

He lifted his chin ridiculously high and looked down his nose at her.

Paris tried not to laugh. "That's only funny when you do it."

"Or when you do it without even knowing you're doing it." He ran a finger gently down the length of her nose, and she felt herself go into meltdown. "I thought you did it deliberately, just because it bugged the hell out of me."

"I guess it's become a habit."

"It's not you."

"What do you mean?" She pulled at a loose thread in

the mat. "How can you know what's me or not me when *I* haven't a clue?"

"You've more clues than you give yourself credit for."

Her heart lurched drunkenly in response to both the faint praise and his warmly indulgent tone. But she kept her gaze firmly fixed on the loose thread and tugged harder. "How do you mean?"

"I said no to any sort of a relationship, but you kept at me."

The thread snapped in her fingers. Her gaze flew to his. *Don't read too much into this,* she told herself, but her ever-hopeful heart didn't listen. It turned huge somersaults within her constricting rib cage. With infinite care she constructed her next question. "Does this mean you've changed your answer?"

"Taking the last half hour into account, that's a safe assumption."

All right...Paris thought cautiously above the exuberant pounding of her heart. *Time for a little more directness.* "You said you didn't want to sleep with me."

"No." He tapped her on the knee. "You weren't paying attention. I said I didn't have time to be involved with you."

"Oh.... And has that changed?"

"It will. I'm working on it." He frowned, and Paris didn't like that look, or his lack of elaboration. But what could she do? How could she make her availability more obvious without sacrificing her entire supply of pride? The memory of her recent abandonment, how she'd begged and pleaded while he retained perfect control, caused her to prickle anew.

"When you do work it out, do you suppose you can let me know? Send a memo or something?"

"You'll be the first to know."

"Any hint of a time frame? It's only that I seem to have some trouble in getting you to answer my messages."

He had the audacity to laugh again. "Let me guess…that's what the snappy 'Of course' was about earlier, when I said I only had five minutes."

"Well, you have been avoiding me, haven't you?"

He scrubbed a hand across his face. "Yes."

"Why?"

"Because I knew I'd eventually end up with you underneath me." He looked around ruefully. "Somewhere inappropriate." He released a long sigh, which seemed to chase all the amusement from his eyes. "I'm supposed to be looking after you, not *going* after you."

She couldn't help smiling at his choice of words, even though her stomach dipped and churned. He was about to tell her all about strings again, about her being the boss's daughter, and his responsibility to his boss, and that reminded her of why he was the wrong man for her. It also reminded her of her responsibility to her job and to achieving some respect. "You're right," she admitted, surprising him.

"No argument?"

How to explain? "Today I had a revelation of sorts." She started slowly, hoping she didn't sound too corny or melodramatic. "I realized how important this job is to me, how much I want to succeed. And today I finally felt I'd made some progress. Julie actually made a joke."

She smiled at the perplexed look on his face and made a dismissive gesture.

"Believe me, that's a sign I've made progress…. But I could so easily have undone all that good work here, just now." She gestured widely, taking in him, her, the floor, the glass wall.

He leaned forward. Positioned a hand on each of her

hips. Looked right into her eyes as if he could see right into her head. "Is that why you tried to run away before? To protect your reputation? It matters so much to you?"

She nodded, speechless because he was so close.

His eyes developed a wicked gleam. "That hot sex you mentioned...I guess I can forget about your desk?"

Gulp.

"And mine?" He leaned closer and kissed her hard on her mouth. "Pity."

Then, in one athletic movement he pushed to his feet, extended a hand and pulled her up after him. Still reeling from the desk thing, and the kiss, she stumbled onto his toes and needed to steady herself with a hand flat against his chest. The lush rhythm of his heartbeat seemed to permeate her skin, to seep into her blood.

"You want to leave this till after hours, that's fine by me."

He grinned as if he knew how easily he'd turned her inside out, how easily he could have her wherever and however he chose. If he ever chose...

He turned her wrist over, studied her watch, stunned her by asking, "Do you have a car?"

"I'm driving one of K.G.'s."

"The Porsche? I've seen it downstairs. Thought you might be driving it."

She nodded, still struggling to catch up with his latest conversational twist.

"Good. I need a lift."

Paris bristled. Not because she didn't want to drive him, but because he'd presumed, and because she'd never planned on being so easy. "And what if I have other plans?"

"Then you needn't stay for dinner."

With that he turned and headed for the shower, leaving

Paris standing in the middle of the gym floor, a dumb smile curving her lips and happiness seeping through her body, turning it into one sorry mushy mess. It didn't seem to matter how much she cautioned herself, remembering the hurry he'd been in to get out of here, as if he already had an appointment. Only one thing mattered.

Jack was taking her to dinner.

Yes!

Eight

Not only dinner with Jack, but dinner at Jack's house!

That startling news, calmly delivered as she negotiated the Porsche out of Grantham's underground car park, caused Paris's foot to spasm on the accelerator, launching them into heavy traffic with perilous speed. From the corner of her eye she saw Jack's hand braced rigidly on the dashboard. She didn't blame him. Her own heart was pounding extravagantly from the near miss. If she kept this up she would never get to enjoy The First Date.

That thought almost caused her to hyperventilate. She needed to relax, to focus on something other than what awaited at the end of the drive, else she would never get them safely there. With a brilliant flash of recall, she fastened on why she'd come to the gym in the first place.

Telling Jack about her plans for the Landing Launch, as she'd christened it, soon occupied both her mind and the hands she needed to stress every second point.

"I'm glad you only need to talk with one hand at a time," Jack commented dryly.

She flashed him an old-fashioned look, but spoiled it with the smile she didn't seem able to lose. "I suppose you're one of those chicken-livered people who prefer driving with one hand on the wheel?"

"A minimum requirement."

She pulled a face and watched him undo his top button. "You hate wearing a collar and tie, don't you?"

"Doesn't everyone?"

She glanced across at him, smiling. "K.G. was born wearing one."

"Now there's a picture." He grinned back at her, and for a moment they were caught in the intimacy of their shared amusement—until a car horn blared. She swiftly corrected her steering.

"Maybe I should have taken a taxi."

She laughed and executed a tricky lane change with considerable style. "You don't trust me?"

"Sweetheart, I don't trust anyone who drives a car like this."

Sweetheart. Oh, if only... Ruthlessly she shoved the silent longing aside, determined not to spoil things by wishing for too much. "Why am I driving you, by the way? What's wrong with your tank?"

"Nothing. My sister borrowed it. *Her* European status symbol stood her up this afternoon."

"Tina," Paris recalled from her conversation with Julie. Out loud, apparently, because Jack inspected her with one brow quirked.

"You've met Tina?"

Oh, help! How to explain this one? She pretended to concentrate on an unnecessary lane change while she framed her answer. Ultimately she chose the truth. "I saw you together this afternoon, from my window. Julie told me she was your sister.''

"You asked Julie?''

"Not exactly.'' Feeling foolish, she mumbled, "It came up.''

He seemed to take a long time assimilating that. Under the pretext of checking traffic, she chanced a peek his way and wondered why he should look so pleased with himself. As if he'd read her thoughts, he leaned closer and asked, "Did it come up because you saw me with another woman? Because you had to know about her?''

Paris squirmed, until he slid a large warm hand onto her knee. Then she simply melted into the seat. Close to her ear, he purred, "Were you jealous, princess? Did it eat at you from the inside out?''

Yes, she thought, mesmerized by his low, velvet voice and the slow caress of his hand above her knee.

"Because that's exactly how I felt about you and Teddy.''

Paris swallowed convulsively. Did he mean he'd thought about her while she was with Edward? Or only when she'd spoken of him at the Landing? She longed to ask, needing it to be the first as much as she needed her next breath, but dreading his answer, knowing it would be the second. She didn't ask. Several kilometers passed in a silence that felt heavy with the unasked, the unsaid, the unacknowledged. Finally she could bear it no longer. She cleared her throat.

"Where do you live?''

She'd wanted to say something else—to caution him about the possessiveness, no doubt. He'd seen the worry churning across her face and instantly regretted revealing so much, too soon. When she'd revealed nothing.

"Well?'' she prompted.

"Orchard Hills.''

She shook her head slowly, her face blank. Obviously she'd never heard of the unpretentious outer suburb that suited him perfectly. Did they have anything in common beyond the raging itch to get horizontal? Beyond Grantham House? The thought bothered him. He withdrew his hand from her leg. Perhaps he'd jumped the gun bringing her home. Too much, too soon.

Too late.

His exit came up quickly, and he directed her to the left lane and off the freeway, around two turns, into Grevillea Drive. Both her hands gripped the wheel tightly, as if in heightened anticipation. Or apprehension.

"Slow down," he directed as they approached his driveway. "Here. This one."

The car skidded as she cornered too quickly, narrowly missing a pair of solid timber gate posts. Paris held her breath until the tires grabbed asphalt again. She barely had time to register the size of the property when a pack of dogs with no respect for wheels or cars or mortality careened out of the trees. She stood on the brake and the Porsche slewed sideways, spewing up gravel before kangaroo-hopping to a stop.

"You okay?"

She nodded. It seemed like half the canine population of western Sydney was circling the car in a mad, yapping frenzy.

"I suspect you'll find room to park closer to the house," he suggested dryly.

Paris gestured at the marauding pack. "If I keep driving I'll run over them."

"They'll get out of your way."

She swung around to face him. "I've got a better idea. You get out of the car and get your lunatic dogs under control!"

One eyebrow quirked. "I would if I could, but they're not mine."

"Whose are they?"

Jack squinted out the window. With the initial canine excitement abating, Paris noted there were fewer individuals than she'd thought.

"The big stupid-looking one belongs to my sister Anna. Which means there'll be a Jack Russell somewhere, property of her kids. The beagle having trouble keeping up is Mum's, and the rough-looking mongrel is brother Mike's. I think that's about it."

"Oh." The implications sank in. There was more than the one sister Julie mentioned. Jack had a large *family* family. "Who lives here, exactly?" she asked, peering through the trees beside the driveway. Like the dogs, the trees came in all shapes and sizes and varieties. Through them she could just make out the outline of a large house.

"Myself, naturally. Plus, at the moment—" he used his fingers to count off "—there's Mum, Mike and my youngest sister, Libby, although she's never home. After Dad died last year, Mum decided to sell up and build something smaller. In the meantime, she moved in here. The dregs who can't cook for themselves followed."

Paris nodded as if she understood, which of course she didn't...unless his family was very like Marge's. She started the engine and was about to select a gear when a group of children streamed across the road in the distance. The dogs took off in noisy pursuit.

"Exactly how big is your family?" she asked slowly.

"Two brothers, three sisters. Those," he gestured toward the disappearing children, "call me Uncle Jack."

Paris unwrapped her hands from the wheel and wiped her palms on her Armani skirt.

"Hey, they're not so scary. Noisy, but not scary," he said gently.

It was an obvious attempt to humor her, but Paris didn't feel like being humored. He hadn't mentioned family. She never would have agreed to come if he'd mentioned family.

"You told me once you wished you had a big family." As if he'd been reading her mind again.

"Yes, well, you can't order one of those out of a catalog."

She hated her snippy tone, hated the confusion she felt, because she had no idea why she felt so overwhelmed. She shoved the car into gear and drove on to the house. And of course it was nothing like she'd expected, either.

What had started life as a simple A-frame had been extended with unstructured abandon. The timber—western red cedar, she suspected—was relieved only by vast expanses of glass. Right off she knew it wasn't a house. It was a home.

The car was surrounded again, this time by a mixture of whooping and yapping. Above the hubbub she could hear distinct cries of "Uncle Jack, Uncle Jack!"

Uncle Jack put his hand over one of hers on the wheel. "Feeling up to meeting a few Mannings?"

The panicky feeling swamped her again. It wasn't that she didn't want to see his home and meet his family, it was just that she felt unready and uncertain and too much like the woman who'd come apart under Jack's hand an hour before.

How could she look his mother in the eye?

She took a deep quivering breath. "No offence, but I don't think this is a good time. I mean, they're not expecting me and I'm not dressed for meeting mothers and this is a family thing—and don't say I can have a drink because I can't drink when I'm driving—"

"You're babbling."

Paris bit the inside of her lip. Yes, she was babbling, when she would be better off thinking up a decent excuse. "I'd love to come in, Jack, but I've just remembered that Felicity is coming up tonight." A lie, and a lame one at that.

"Who's Felicity?" he asked.

"An old school friend who I've just found out lives in the same apartment building, two floors down." At least that much was the truth.

"If she lives that close, then she won't mind taking a rain check."

"No, I suppose not." Paris searched for a better excuse. "But I did forget to water my plants." Equally lame, as the plants weren't likely to die in the next few hours. She retrieved her mobile phone from her bag. "I'll ring."

"The plants?"

"Felicity."

His big dark hand closed over the phone, took it from her limp hand. One finger turned her face and made her look at him. "They don't bite."

Past his shoulder, several small faces pressed against the window. At least one had teeth. "You should have told me, let me get used to the idea."

"Would you have come?"

She didn't answer.

"That's what I thought." He paused. "I want you to come in, but I understand if you can't. I can take that rain check."

She bit her lip again. Felt suffocated by his closeness, by those earnest little faces, by something inside she couldn't name. "I really do have to ring Felicity. You go ahead. I'll come in when I'm finished."

For a long breath-held minute she thought he had more

to say, but then he kissed her on her forehead, said "No need to knock, come right on in," and let himself out of the car.

Through the tinted windscreen she saw him pick up a little girl and throw her high in the air. Her squeal of delight pierced the din. An even smaller boy attached himself to Jack's leg—he made a great show of trying to walk with the attachment, limping up the steps as if he had a heavily weighted wooden leg. The biggest of the dogs—she couldn't recall who it belonged to—jumped all about the little party, a long pink tongue hanging limply from the side of its grinning mouth.

Oh my! Paris put a hand to her mouth, as if that might contain her crazily bounding heart. What was wrong with her? Why wasn't she out the door, bounding up those steps beside him? Wasn't this exactly what she'd dreamed of, to be invited into Jack's home, to be included in his life?

The low growl of the idling engine reverberated through her nerve endings, encouraging her to leave. She engaged the clutch and pushed the gear-stick from position to position, finally selecting first. Cowardly, yes, but how could she walk into his house, filled with his family, unannounced? How could she... She jumped clean out of her seat when the passenger door reopened, revealing a dark-haired toddler. Hand on thudding heart, she watched the tot climb onto the passenger seat, slip a dirty thumb into her mouth and stare up at her with huge eyes the exact same cola-brown as Jack's.

Help, thought Paris, and she repeated the silent plea as she looked out and noted the emptiness. Where had they all gone? It seemed that even the dogs had deserted her.

She inspected her silent companion for a moment. "Why don't you go inside, honey? I'm sure your mother's wondering where you are."

"Honey" didn't move.

"I have to go home now, so you'll have to get out of my car."

The big dark eyes widened slightly, and the thumb slipped from her open mouth. "My name's not Honey. It's Dat," she said with solemn condemnation.

"What an unusual name. Is it short for something?"

The big dark eyes stared back at her.

Paris smiled helplessly and extended her hand. "Well, hello, Dat. I'm very pleased to meet you. My name's Paris."

Dat inspected the hand but didn't take it, so Paris leaned closer and gave her the same solemn-eyed look. "I really have to go now, Dat. How about you hop out?"

Dat shook her head, and her thick dark curls rioted about her face. Paris looked about again. No rescue party in sight. With a resigned sigh she turned off the engine and held out her arms. It took all of five seconds before a pair of pudgy and far-from-clean arms fastened themselves around her neck. Paris accepted the stranglehold as she slid from the car, but when the warm little face buried itself in her neck she stopped stock-still.

She inhaled the delicate scent of baby shampoo and ran a hand over the untidy mop that tickled her jaw. Her heart lurched uncomfortably when one of Dat's sticky hands mimicked the action.

"You'f dot nice hair," Dat said.

"Thank you. And so have you." Paris swallowed a furball of remembered emotion. It was more than ten years since she'd last held a child like this.

She shook away the memory and took the three steps onto the wide verandah, knocked on the screen door, hovered, peered into the house. Voices, the hum of adult conversation and the squeals of children, drifted out from somewhere within. She knocked more loudly and tried to disengage Dat's hands from around her neck. The little arms tightened their grip.

"Uncle Jack did say 'Come on in,' didn't he, Datkin," she muttered as she made her way gingerly into the house and through an entrance foyer in search of...*anyone.*

Nine

It wasn't hard to find someone. Paris gravitated toward the sound of many voices—not the low hum of conversation but loud, uninhibited voices. Before she could register more than the noise factor, a familiar redhead appeared in front of her, said "There you are," and whipped Dat out of her arms. She threw Paris an openly inquisitive look and a friendly "Hello" before disappearing up a staircase.

Paris took a deep breath and stepped into the room. The noise didn't exactly stop—somewhere overhead children squealed, while a kitchen appliance buzzed in the next room—but in front of her the conversation ground to a halt.

Jack was leaning against the bar, his back to the door, but he knew who had stopped the conversation even before Mike whistled low between his teeth and groaned, "Mercy." He reminded himself that Mike was family, therefore he shouldn't want to enact violence upon him.

Carefully he placed his beer on the bar, and just as carefully he said, "Hands off, little brother. The lady's mine."

She stood just inside the door, back straight, chin high, her eyes filled with a mute appeal. *Help me!* The odd mix of dignity and insecurity grabbed him hard. He wanted to charge across the room, to claim her, protect her. Before he could make it halfway, Vince was pressing a beer into her hand.

Anna rolled her eyes in disbelief. "Did you think to ask if she wanted something more civilized, Vincent?" She eyed Jack's approach with bright-eyed curiosity. "Aren't you going to introduce your girlfriend, Jackboot?"

Jack shot his sister a *can it!* glare, just as his mother came through from upstairs with at least six grandchildren in tow.

"Now they're all washed up, we can sit down to eat." She stopped and smiled at Paris. "Hello, dear. Did you drive Jack home? I hope you can stay for tea. It's nothing special, but you're very welcome."

Paris opened her mouth to answer, but his mother was already bustling off to the kitchen, talking over her shoulder.

"Jack, you can introduce your friend after we sit down. If you don't come through now it will be spoiled."

Jack waited until they'd all disappeared before he turned to Paris. Eyes wide, she breathed a "Phew" of relief or bewilderment or released tension. Or maybe all three, he figured. He smoothed her hair back behind one ear and stroked the side of her neck. "You didn't run away." Until the moment she'd appeared in the doorway, he hadn't realized how important that was to him.

"I'm only here because some little ragamuffin railroaded me."

"Aah, that would be Dat."

"Strange name."

"Long story. Natalie shortened to Nat, which her brother couldn't say, thus Dat." He pressed a quick kiss to her neck and enjoyed the way her eyes glazed over. "She's working undercover for me. I hoped she might persuade you to stay."

"She's something."

"I'm glad you like her." He bent and nuzzled her ear. "I'm wanting to kiss you other places but if we don't appear soon, they'll send out a search party."

Only two empty chairs remained at his huge slab of a dining table, and they were six places apart. Jack gesticulated at Mike. Mike grinned and stayed put. "Hi," he drawled to Paris. "I'm Mike, Jack's much-better-looking brother. Why don't you sit here next to me?" He patted the chair beside him.

She smiled her killer smile, said "Pleased to meet you," and Jack felt like doing violence again, brother be damned! He wondered how long he would need in her bed to work off these caveman tendencies. He glowered at Mike until his brother moved seats. The women exchanged knowing looks across the table, which Jack studiously ignored. He helped Paris into the chair next to his and reached for the bread basket.

"Where are your manners, Jack Manning?" his mother called from the other end of the table.

Jack put down his roll and leaned closer to Paris, pointing across the table with his bread knife. "Brother Vince you already met. The stunner next to him is his wife Kim. That's Kristina, but we all call her Tina." He used his knife to count them off, one by one. "You can call Mum Mary. We won't worry about all the rug rats this time round. And that's Mike...unfortunately. Then my eldest sister, Anna, and her husband, Deak. Everyone, this is Paris."

Introductions over, they all resumed where they'd left off, which involved a lot of loud talk, reaching across the table, filling of plates and clattering of crockery. Jack's mother—Paris couldn't bring herself to think of her as Mary—made halfhearted attempts at control. Her calls of "Vincent, that was uncalled for" or "Michael, watch your language" didn't actually go unheeded. They were answered with a wry "You weren't supposed to be listening, Mum" or a well-worn "Sorry, Mum."

Despite her initial misgivings, Paris couldn't help but relax. The mood of easy camaraderie and good-natured teasing was infectious. Much of the ribbing involved what Mike called Jack's *alleged* love life, but Jack didn't seem to mind. He didn't correct anyone about her status in his life, and she felt a warm, possessive glow each time her name was linked with his. She also felt a warm glow every time he touched her, which was often. At the moment his arm rested on the back of her chair, his fingers playing absently in the ends of her hair as he discussed some council zoning problem with Deak.

When the women started gathering plates and taking them to the kitchen, Paris followed. It seemed like the thing to do. She found Anna elbow deep in suds and Tina shooing "Mum" with the end of a tea towel. "Go and help Kim with the kids," she said. "They're putting a video on."

"Can I help?" Paris asked tentatively.

Tina slung the tea towel over her shoulder. "Go for it. I'll make coffee."

The first few minutes were tricky, as Anna jumped straight into a subtle inquisition regarding Paris's relationship with Jack. She didn't seem inclined to accept that they "just worked together," but what else could Paris say? *We're about to embark on a hot and steamy affair of indefinite duration* was more than Jack's sister needed to know.

She managed to divert the conversation to safer ground by asking Anna what she did.

"Me? I'm full-time in management," she answered, with a wry smile.

"In what area?"

"Domestic management."

Tina snorted and nudged Paris with an elbow. "She's winding you up. She *thinks* she manages her house and kids, but that's debatable."

"I used to manage the business very efficiently, if you don't mind!" Anna sniffed.

"The business?"

The other two women exchanged a look. "Manning Homes. We all work there. Vince and Deak and Mike do the macho, hammer-and-nails stuff, I look after marketing, and Kim does interior design on the prefabs. Anna used to be office manager." Tina sneered at her sister, who flicked her with soap suds and called her a rude name.

Paris bit her lip. Oh, how she envied their suds-flicking, name-calling closeness. No one ever called Paris Grantham rude names...not to her face, at any rate.

Kim swung into the kitchen to inquire about the coffee shortage, starting a new barrage of raillery. Paris studied the women from beneath lowered lashes. Kim slotted into the family as if she was born to it, yet there must have been a time when she was the outsider. Had she felt this intense need to belong? Had the transition been easy?

"Hey, Kim, Paris is working on Milson Landing. She's likely seen your *pièce de résistance*," Tina called across to her sister-in-law, before turning to Paris. "Have you seen inside Jack's villa? Neat isn't it?"

"It's magic. Did you do the whole place?" she asked Kim.

"Unfortunately." Kim rolled her eyes, but she looked pleased nonetheless. "That is definitely the last job I'm doing for Jack. Talk about limiting one's artistic freedom. That man with his inflexible plans." Kim shuddered.

"I tried to warn you," Anna laughed. "Why d'you think I call him Jackboot?"

Paris smiled at the banter even while a frisson of concern scurried through her system. Inflexible? Surely they exaggerated. He'd changed his mind about her.

"Come on, Paris. Your man might be in need of rescuing." Tina stood poised at the door, a tray of coffee mugs balanced delicately on one hand. "Have they got him in a headlock yet?" she asked Kim.

"Naturally."

What were they talking about?

Paris's bewilderment must have shown, for Kim took pity on her. "Every time the men get together they feel compelled to talk Jack into coming back to Mannings," she explained. "Like he's going to give up his big city job!"

The loud gurgle of draining water punctuated Kim's rolling-eyed denouement, and Anna called over her shoulder, "Glad that's finished. After about the sixtieth plate I'm always wishing I was an only child."

"Never, never wish that on yourself," Paris murmured. Then, afraid someone might have heard the pathetic aside, she hung up her towel and hurried out to the living room.

Jack wasn't in a headlock. He was moving to make room for her on the sofa. "Okay?" he asked.

"I'm fine."

But as soon as she slipped into the space beside him, she knew she'd lied. She felt the security of his big body alongside hers, the weight of his arm draped casually around her shoulders, the play of his fingers in her hair. She absorbed the warmth of Kim's smile as she handed out coffee, the low drone of Vince and Mike's conversation, the laughter of children from another room. She saw the tender kiss Deak pressed on Anna's forehead as she sat on the floor between his knees, and longing grew to a tight choking congestion in her throat, her chest, her heart.

I don't want to be his short-term lover. I want all this. The teasing, the warmth, the intimacy, the family.

The love.

Her mug wobbled in her hand, sloshing coffee over the rim. Jack took the mug and wiped her hand. For some reason he couldn't figure, she looked shell-shocked. Unless it was the upshot of being trapped in the kitchen with his sisters for the last half hour. Hell! He shouldn't have let her go in there; he should have known they would give her a hard time.

"If you've all finished being free with my food and drink—" he yawned widely and suggestively "— I'm thinking about an early night." But no one took the hint, except the one guest he didn't want leaving. She jumped straight to her feet.

"Yes," she piped. "I'd best be going. I didn't mean to stay so long."

Jack glared his narrow-eyed disapproval at every sibling and sibling-in-law he could establish eye contact with. They ignored him. He managed to extricate Paris before his mother could press a plate of leftovers into her hands and was about to escort her somewhere private when a small missile launched herself at their legs. He looked down to see Dat attaching herself to the hem of Paris's skirt. Jack scooped her up in one arm and shook his head. "Aren't you supposed to be watching *Anastasia,* Natalie Kate Deakin?"

"I'f seen it six times." She held up four chocolaty fingers, tossed off a dimple-cheeked grin and wound her arms around his neck. The kid might be a bit rusty on the counting, but she had all the moves down pat. Then, past her curls, he saw his mother fussing over the handprints on Paris's skirt.

"It doesn't matter. Really." She gave the marks a cursory brush. "It's only a skirt."

"It's a bloody sensational skirt," Anna interjected. "I'd kill to get into something like that."

Mike grinned and said, "So would I."

Jack thought, I'm going to kill every last one of them. Slowly and painfully. Starting with Mike.

When he finally steered her out the door, they were pursued by calls of "Come again" and "Don't be a stranger."

Who owns this place, anyway?

He made a mental note to speak to Vince about finishing his mother's house. *Yesterday.*

He trailed her to the Porsche and leaned against the driver's door. There was enough light from the porch and the three-quarter moon to see her face, but not enough to gauge her mood. Back there on the sofa she'd seemed edgy, and she'd been in a mighty hurry to leave. He shuffled Dat in his arms. "Sorry about all that."

"All what? If you mean the skirt, it doesn't matter. I only have about a hundred of them."

"Which doesn't mean you have to put up with my nieces mauling them."

"Are you apologizing for your family?" She peered closely at him; he bounced Dat back to his other arm. "You are. You're apologizing." She shook her head slowly.

"God, Jack, what I wouldn't give to have a family like yours!"

Her pronouncement hung in the still night air, startling them both with its passion.

"I thought—" Hell, what did he think? "I didn't want you to feel uncomfortable."

"I *did* feel uncomfortable, but it wasn't your fault or your family's. They're great." She smiled, but it was a sad, crooked effort, as poignant as her earlier statement.

What I wouldn't give to have a family like yours.

"They have their moments.... I guess you haven't played happy families much."

"Granthams don't play families, full stop." She took a shaky breath. "We had a housekeeper, though. Marge. She had a terrific family, a lot like yours."

"I remember her. Nice lady. Great chocolate chip cookies."

"That's Marge." Her smile didn't reach her eyes. "She used to take me to her place sometimes, on weekends, school holidays. God, I loved her place. I used to wish I could—" She looked down, scuffed at the ground with the toe of one sandal. "Earlier on, when Dat put her arms around my neck, I remembered how Emily used to do that. She was their youngest, a late baby. Marge used to call her 'the best surprise we've ever had.'" She looked up, eyes large in her shadowy face. Her tight little smile twisted Jack's gut. "I used to pretend she was my little sister."

"Do you ever see them?"

Paris shook her head. "Marge died while I was away." She wiped her hands down the sides of her skirt. "I should be going. Let you get back to your family."

"They don't need looking after." *But you do.* If it weren't for Dat, he would have reached for her, cradled her close, done anything to wipe those lonely memories from her eyes, those years of having everything money could buy but nothing a child needed. He didn't want her to go. "Why don't you stay?"

She shook her head, didn't meet his eyes. "No. I couldn't."

Of course she didn't want to stay, not with his house swarming with relatives. "I have spare rooms."

Her eyes flicked to his, surprised. "You're inviting me to stay…in a spare room?" She moistened her lips, considering, deciding, and Jack's body quickened.

"Maybe that's not such a good idea." Without installing heavy duty locks, he couldn't guarantee she would remain alone in that spare room. "What are you doing tomorrow?"

"I don't have anything planned. Why?"

"I've a site inspection at eleven. I could come by and pick you up, if you'd like to come."

She shook her head. "I don't think so."

"You have something against construction sites?"

"Only on weekends."

Hell. Jack balanced his niece in one arm and rubbed the back of his neck. Was it tiredness making him so slow? She'd just finished telling him how she'd spent her childhood weekends with the housekeeper's family because her own mother had done a bunker and her father was too busy adding to his millions.

He could delegate the inspection. "Have you anything against eating on weekends?"

"No."

Jack thought about dinner, but that was more than twenty hours away. Lunch was fourteen. "What's your position on brunch?" he asked.

She cleared her throat, smiled tentatively. "I'm open to negotiations."

"Eleven?"

Her smile widened. "Ten. And I get to choose where."

"Ten-thirty," he said, but only to show it wouldn't be all *her* way. "And I do the choosing. That's my final offer."

Her eyes narrowed. "Fine, but it would be remiss of me not to tell you about this little place—"

Jack silenced negotiations by kissing her. He took his own sweet time, felt the gentle movement of her lips under his, the giving softness of her mouth. She tasted of warm coffee and even warmer promises, and by the time he lifted his face from hers, he felt pretty certain they'd come to agreeable terms.

He was about to make sure when Dat tugged at his hair. He bounced her upright. "Tired, bunny?"

She nodded.

"Then you'd better kiss Paris good-night and we'll go tell your parents to get you home to bed." He rubbed his cheek against Dat's until she batted him away.

"You stratch," she said, pouting.

Paris's smile turned wicked. "And we don't like men who scratch, do we, Dat?" She took a step closer and stroked his whiskery jaw with the palm of her hand. Her shadowy eyes and black-silk voice stroked him in other places.

Tomorrow, Jack told his impatient body. And only after we've talked, settled a few things. He pushed far enough off the car to open the door, but not far enough that she couldn't slide by without major body contact. As she dragged her hips slowly past his with a whispery, "Excuse me," he wondered when he'd developed masochistic tendencies.

He shut the door behind her and tapped the window with his knuckles. It slithered open. "Forgetting something?"

Her eyes crossed as he dropped a slow kiss on the tip of her nose. "Your address."

She rummaged about in her bag, scribbled for a moment, then handed him a folded piece of paper. "It's not too difficult to find. Buzz me at the car-park gate and I'll let you in. Finding a place to park on the street can be a real problem."

He stepped back as the window whirred shut and the engine purred to life. He cradled Dat's sleepy head against his shoulder and didn't move until the thrum of expensive European engineering faded in the night air. The thrum in his blood played on long after he strapped Dat into her car seat and waved the last of his "guests" goodbye. It kept him awake, hard and restless between heated sheets, into the early morning. But he didn't regret sending her home or not coaxing her to stay.

He needed time to grab hold of his impulses, to formulate a strategy for tomorrow—one that took into account everything that had changed in the last five hours…and the one thing that hadn't. She was still Paris Grantham, the boss's daughter. She didn't know it yet, but he intended to give her everything she'd missed out on.

It was as simple and as complex as that.

Ten

"Oh, sheesh!" Paris glared at the gouge in her freshly painted fingernail, then at the dead bolt responsible. If she had X-ray vision she would also be glaring at the person pounding on her door at eight in the morning.

"Hold on, Felicity. I'm trying to get it!" Preferably without messing up any more of these nails. "You don't happen to know a decent manicurist who works on a Saturday morn..." Her voice trailed off as the door swung open.

It wasn't Felicity.

It was Jack. He was hours too early, and he looked divine. The tobacco chambray shirt highlighted the deeper warmth of his eyes and hugged his broad chest. The well-worn jeans highlighted his long legs and hugged all kinds of other interesting places. Just looking at him caused her breath to catch, her pulse to thud and her bare toes to curl into the carpet.

"You were expecting someone else?" His gaze strolled from her towel-wrapped hair to her freshly exfoliated face and on to the short-sleeved Mizrahi knit she'd washed on hot cycle. His leisurely inspection halted somewhere around her middle, presumably where the shrunken cardigan didn't quite meet her oldest pair of jeans.

"Not expecting. I assumed it would be Felicity, seeing as she's the only person I know in this building and anyone else would need to get through security."

He held up a security card. "Lucky I have an interest in this building."

Of course. Paris rolled her eyes. *He probably built the place!*

She was about to ask, then noticed his attention drift back to her middle region. It should have peeved her, except she didn't want him staring with such intensity at her face, which was probably all red and blotchy from the mask.

She crossed her arms over her tightening breasts and wondered how bolting to her bedroom to change into something less obvious, something with a bra under it, would be interpreted.

"Aren't you going to invite me in?" He stepped around her before she could answer. "Why are you holding your hands like that?"

"Because you're early!" She held her hands out so he could see the interrupted manicure.

Because at six I gave up trying to get back to sleep and I needed something to occupy myself, else I'd go crazy. I started with the face stuff, because I looked so haggard from spending the whole night tossing and turning, consumed by the enormity of what I feel for you and want from you, when all there's going to be is a hot time in bed.

Annoyed with herself as much as him, Paris humphed into the living room and plopped down on the sofa. She unwound the towel from her still-damp hair and dragged a comb through the mess while she struggled to deal with her massive anxiety attack.

Jack's early arrival must mean he'd changed his mind about brunch. The on-site appointment had taken precedence. Of course. She picked up the nail polish and shook the bottle viciously.

The softly sprung sofa dipped under his weight, and Paris straightened her posture to stop herself from pitching toward him—not because she felt defensive. To prove her point, she asked politely, "Why is it you're here so early?"

Jack smothered a smile. She was trying so hard to act cool but failing miserably. "I heard you needed a manicurist."

She started working at her nails, but the angry little dabs were an exercise in futility.

He smiled despite himself. "Here, you're making it worse," he said, reaching for her hands. A mild tug-of-war ensued before she gave in and let him place them, wrists down, across his knee. He clicked finger against thumb. "Give."

She handed over the cotton bud.

"Remover." She threw a mutinous look, then the bottle. Jack caught both easily before surveying her earlier work. The left hand wasn't too bad, but the three fingers she'd attempted on the right hand were woeful. "I can see why you need a professional," he remarked dryly.

When he'd removed the damaged polish, she thanked him and reclaimed her hands. Patiently he drew them back onto his thigh and picked up the little bottle of polish. "And here I was thinking you'd be a morning person," he said conversationally.

"Mornings are fine once I've had time to put my makeup on," she snapped.

"I'm going to be seeing you in the morning without makeup or anything else on. Get used to it, sweetheart."

She blinked, her mouth fell open, and Jack felt a sweet punch of satisfaction. He'd been right to come early and catch her off guard. From now on he intended upsetting her rhythm on a regular basis—not because he needed to be in control, but because he liked seeing her out of control. The picture she made, all rumpled and off-kilter and touchingly self-conscious, coiled insidiously around his heart. This was the woman he'd hoped to find beneath that picture-perfect facade. This was the woman for him. With a satisfied little smile, he shook the polish, positioned her hands exactly where he wanted them and started painting.

He worked with the same intense focus he employed in the office, Paris noted. *And yesterday in the gym. On the floor of the gym.* Her hand shook with the powerful image invoked by that thought, and he grasped her wrist, held it steady against his thigh. Through the soft denim she could feel his body heat, the strength in his long, hard muscle, and then he bent closer, so close their heads bumped. She inhaled the scent of freshly showered skin, felt a pull as strong as steel to a magnet…and jerked herself clear.

A few strands of hair caught and held, dark amber against black, before they slowly released their tenuous grip and slid away. The sensual imagery was dizzying. Paris wanted to reach for his dark head, to bury her fingers in his hair. She wanted to kiss him and kiss him and kiss him. Everywhere. She wanted…God, she wanted so intensely it scared her.

"All done." He lifted her hands and tilted them in the light, giving a grunt of satisfaction as he inspected the finished product.

The fingers cuffing her wrists might have detected her skittery pulse, or maybe he'd started reading her mind again…whatever the reason, his mood changed. With slow, seductive purpose he bent over her hands and blew gently across her fingertips. Awareness skittered along her nerve endings, until it felt as if he'd peeled her clothes open and puffed that slow, warm breath all over her body.

When he leaned forward, she thought he might kiss her, and oh, how she yearned for that, but he merely lifted her arms one after the other and placed them carefully along the back of the sofa. "Don't want to ruin all my hard work," he explained as he settled back into his corner of the sofa.

Paris blinked, attempting to clear her mind of the heat haze. She couldn't get any sort of grip on his mood this morning. He seemed so unnaturally calm, so even and controlled, and the way he sat there silently inspecting her ate away at her own shaky confidence. She hated this intense scrutiny, hated being so caught out. She needed to brush her hair, fix her face, to know what he was thinking, and why he was in her living room thinking it.…

"You didn't say why you're early," she blurted.

"That's a problem?"

Yes. No. "I'm not ready."

Jack allowed himself the pleasure of appraising both her readiness and her rising temper. He took in the heightened color along her cheekbones, the slight flare of her nostrils, the defensive posture. The way her eyes had darkened to the gunmetal gray of a stormy sky. "You look fine to me."

Better than fine. Her thickly tousled hair looked as if it had just rolled out of bed, and with her arms spreadeagled, the cardigan-thingy did enthralling things to her breasts. She definitely wasn't wearing a bra. His gaze dropped to her middle. Not even a glimpse of the belly button that had greeted him at the door. Too bad.

His eyes took their own good time returning to hers, and

there it was again. That delicious spark of temper. He knew he shouldn't push it, but he couldn't help himself. Leaning closer, he traced a slow path across the back of her hand with his fingertips. She inhaled sharply, and her breasts expanded against the tight top. Jack liked this top. A lot.

"What is it you don't feel ready for?" he asked as he trailed his fingers up her bare forearm and stroked the inside of her elbow with his thumb.

She shivered and moistened her lips. "You... *No!* I mean, going to brunch with you."

The nervous gaffe and her awareness of it, alight in her smoky eyes and the rosy flush of her skin, spoke directly to Jack's hormones. His whole body leaped from three-parts alert to full attention. He eased back, taking his hand with him. If he took it slow and maintained some degree of detachment, he might just manage to stick to his plan—to talk first, eat second, then make love with an element of finesse.

"Before we do brunch, we're going to settle a few things."

"What kind of things?"

"How it's going to be between us." She stared back at him, and the air seemed to crackle with awareness, with what they both knew would happen between them. "Yes. We will end up in bed, but not until after we've talked and eaten and talked some more."

She drew a long audible breath. The color in her cheeks deepened, her eyes narrowed ominously, and he knew it wasn't only the electricity in the air. She was annoyed. "I guess you need to build up your strength."

"Damn right. Once I get you into that bed, we won't be doing anything else for a long, long while. But before we get there, we need to establish some ground rules."

"Ground rules? You want to establish ground rules?" she asked on a rising note of incredulity.

Jack leaned across and lowered her chin with one finger. "Rule one is you leave all those regal airs and graces at the bedroom door. Rule two is we leave everything Grantham in that same place. Rule three is—"

"What if I won't play by your rules?" she snapped.

"Which one do you object to?"

"I object to the concept. I detest rules."

"Only because you've never had any to follow," he replied evenly.

Was he for real? How could he look at her and touch her as he had, winding her senses into unbearable knots of need, then calmly sit back and start reciting rules? Did he think she was one of his projects, something to plan out step by step?

This is the way it's going to be.

We will end up in bed.

Propelled by her festering chagrin and discomfort—she couldn't believe she was sitting here, her shoulders aching from holding her arms in this ridiculous position so she wouldn't ruin his hard work, for heaven's sake!—Paris surged to her feet. "Tell me, Jack. Amongst all your 'we will do this, we won't do that,' is there any place for what I might want?"

"What *do* you want?"

His voice was so even, so annoyingly calm, it sent Paris's temper right over the edge. Hands on hips, she glared down at him. And lied. "I told you. Sex. Hot, uncomplicated, *no-rules* sex."

"No."

She lifted her chin. "Then I think you'd better leave. This isn't going to work."

He didn't answer, didn't move, except for the flicker of

a muscle in his cheek. And something in his eyes changed. They seemed to glow with dark purpose.

"Do you really want me to leave?" he asked, his voice a low velvet-cloaked murmur that turned her skin all hot and tight. His gaze held hers captive, so intent and direct that she swore he could see right into her mind. She didn't need to answer. He knew. The firm set look on his face softened. One corner of his mouth quirked up. "Come here," he said gently. Patted the seat beside him.

She sat, and was pulled onto his lap so swiftly that all the air left her lungs in a whoosh.

"That's better. Now pay attention, sweetheart. I'm only going to say this once." He traced the outline of her mouth with his thumb. His voice sounded the same as his thumb felt. All rough-edged sense-tuning magic. She fought against it, truly she did, but it was like swimming against the tide. She summoned her strength for one last objection.

"Is this about rules again?"

"No. This is about us." The thumb traced her cheek-bone. "Once we make love, there will be strings. There'll be no more talk about low-maintenance relationships and affairs that might fizzle out. None of that was ever going to happen. You understand?" His thumb tapped the corner of her mouth.

No, she didn't understand. What sort of relationship did he have in mind? Dare she hope…? Her heart hammered a heavy tattoo as if it, too, had been fighting the tide. She opened her mouth to ask, and his thumb slipped inside. It was accidental, absolutely unintentional, but it was also incredibly evocative. Slowly, experimentally, her lips closed around him, and his breath caught harsh in his throat.

She licked the pad in one long slow sweep, and Jack forgot about talking and eating, about rules and control. He forgot everything the instant he sank into her warm wet mouth. He couldn't stop himself touching her any more than he could stop himself breathing. Her breast pushed full and ripe against his palm, the nipple hard as teak. When he stroked it between his fingers, rolled his thumb across its taut point, she groaned around his thumb. The sensation shot directly to his groin.

He'd never turned so hard, so quickly. His arousal begged for the same slow wet caress, clamored for release. He needed to grab some control—fast. He reclaimed his thumb, and she whispered, "Kiss me," so he did. On her lips, inside her mouth, her earlobe, her throat, and the fever raced like wildfire through his blood.

His fingers trembled and fumbled with the buttons on her top. "What kind of sadist made this thing?" he grumbled.

She laughed low in her throat. "You could just tear it off me."

He didn't need to. The last buttons gave way to an insistent tug, and her head rolled back with abandoned sensuality. For an instant Jack sat perfectly still, overwhelmed by her beauty, needing to feast on it, to fill his eyes and his mind with the image. But only for an instant. Then he had to touch, to taste, to fill his hands and his mouth and his senses. He needed to taste her skin, to feel that fine-grained texture against his tongue, against his own skin. He needed to hear her soft murmurs of encouragement, to feel her hands on him.

He tore at her jeans; she ripped at his shirt. The sound of buttons skidding and spinning on the timber floor was unnaturally loud. Maybe because his senses were more attuned than they'd ever been, maybe because time was suspended.

He slid his fingers inside her open jeans and found her slick heat, and she whimpered the urgency of her need into his mouth. Raw aching desire gripped him hard. He could barely breathe. Her hand at his waist, she tugged at his jeans. There was a fierce savagery in her eyes, and he expected her first touch to be the same. He craved it.

But she touched him with soft, gentle hands, as if he was some precious work of art. Her eyes glazed, her cheeks flushed, her moist lips formed an ''Oh'' of reverent awe, and Jack was caught by a strange ambivalence.

He wanted to slam her onto her back, to surge into her, to erase everything, every man, every touch, that had gone before, to fill her body with only himself. And he wanted to ease it out so the long, lazy, slow-motion kaleidoscope of sensation never ended.

Then she dragged her thumb across the top of his arousal with that same wondrous touch, and his control shredded into paper-thin fragments. He tipped her from his lap and followed her down onto the sofa. Next time he would think about slow, and the time after that, but this time he had to be inside her.

Right now.

He dragged her jeans and panties down her legs and touched her again in her warm slick heat. Caressed her. Until she lifted her hips and opened herself to him. He thrust inside in one swift hard stroke. Stilled. Felt the stunning caress, so tight and wet and sweet around him. And the pleasure was so intense, so furnace hot, he couldn't slow himself...not when she rose to meet him, her long legs wrapped around him, drawing him closer and deeper, until he thought the fire and the need and the urgency might consume him.

And just when he thought he might leave her behind, he leaned down and licked her nipple, twirled his tongue around its lush point, and she shattered around him, plunging them both over the edge of pleasure and pain into the purest ecstasy.

Eleven

Paris floated gently down to earth…or, to be more precise, the living room floor. She still tingled in the most extraordinary places. The arches of her feet, behind her knees, the very tips of her fingers. Oh, and the obvious one, that place at the center of her being.

So this is the afterglow, she thought, with a grin that bordered on smug. All that time with Edward there had never been so much as an afterglimmer. She felt wonderful, all powerful, relaxed and exhilarated at the same time. She wriggled her toes and wondered how long afterglow lasted. At this moment the rest of her life seemed a major possibility.

She started to stretch but found the task nigh impossible, with one arm and both legs pinned under an awful lot of hard-muscled man. Not that she was complaining. No sir! She welcomed the lax male weight as readily as she'd welcomed its taut state earlier.

Taut, she recalled, and wild and spontaneous and intense. So unlike a man following the rules. Her smile curled outward, upward, inward. Concerned it bordered on a smirk, she opened one eye cautiously. Feeling smug was one thing, being caught looking smug was another entirely.

His eyes were still closed. Thick black lashes fanned in twin crescents above his high cheekbones, and, unable to resist, she lifted her free hand to gently trace the furrows between his brows. Today they didn't seem quite so deeply riven.

He tensed, eyes scrunched tight for a second. ''Tell me we didn't just do that,'' he muttered.

Paris gave up trying to control the smirk. ''Oh, I'm pretty sure we did.''

His eyes opened and met hers. They were dark as cola, wary, troubled. Paris lost the smirk. Hadn't it been as spectacular for him? She was no expert but she'd been pretty sure it had.

''Is this about you skipping a few points in the master plan?'' she wondered out loud.

His lips tightened. Then he rolled away from her and spent too many long, silent moments getting into his jeans. His hands jerked roughly at the waist snap, and after three attempts he gave up and sat down on the floor, his back against the sofa.

Sprawled out on the floor in the bright morning light, Paris suddenly felt very naked. She grabbed the closest item of clothing—his shirt—and pulled it on. There were no buttons. Had she ripped it from his body without undoing them? She didn't remember that. She didn't remember getting from the sofa to the floor, either, but that was where they'd ended up.

Betraying warmth crept into her cheeks, but she wasn't about to give in to embarrassment. She would brazen this out, act cool and poised, as if making wild, abandoned love on the living room floor was something she did every other day. She wrapped his shirt close around her body, lifted her chin and met his uneasy gaze.

"I didn't use any protection," he said tightly.

Paris measured her response to this thunderbolt. She couldn't believe she hadn't thought, hadn't noticed.... She couldn't believe she felt so calm about it.

No, not calm.

Jack, the man with all the rules, had been so out of control, so eager, so hot for her, that he'd overlooked the most crucial ground rule. A totally inappropriate sense of elation fizzed through her veins.

"If you're worried about the pregnancy angle, there's no need. I stayed on the pill because it suits my hormones." Somehow she managed to sound matter-of-fact.

"That's not the only consideration."

"I know." Paris straightened her spine with as much dignity as her current position allowed. "I was getting to the second. Edward was always meticulous about things like that. Always."

"And the others?"

"What others?"

He stared at her, shook his head slowly, as if he didn't get her meaning.

She met his eyes levelly. "Edward is the only other man I've slept with."

His eyes darkened to almost black, intense with some emotion she couldn't place. Then he shook his head again. "That's not the point. The point is I didn't even think, *dammit!*" He raked a hand roughly through his hair. "This wasn't how it was supposed to be."

"Ahh, the plan. The ground rules."

His whole face seemed to tighten. "Aren't you even interested in *my* history? About what you might have just exposed yourself to?''

No. Inappropriately and irresponsibly, but definitely no. She closed the gap between them and hunkered down beside him, her hands on his knees. Her answer was simple and straight from her still-glowing heart. ''I trust you.''

''Based on what?''

''Your sense of responsibility.''

He grabbed her face, held it firmly between his hands. ''Oh, yes. I've just acted very responsibly.''

''Based on your reaction, then.'' She placed her hands over his where they held her and met his blazing intensity head-on. ''If this is something you did regularly, I think you'd be a little less outraged, a whole lot less harsh on yourself.''

A storm of emotions roiled behind the midnight patina of his eyes. ''This is the first time I've not used a condom,'' he admitted finally.

''Ever?''

''Ever.''

Paris eased in closer and gently stroked her hands over his. The words she wanted to say formed on her tongue. *I love you.* But did he feel anything for her? Earlier he'd said ''There will be strings,'' but what did that mean? Strings came in a multitude of varieties, including those thin weak-fibered ones that snap under the slightest stress.

She swallowed her words of love and forced out a teasing smile. ''Not even the first time? Not even as a hormonally challenged teenager?''

''Not even way back then.'' The tension in his jaw eased a fraction, and the troubled look in his eyes softened to concern. His hands beneath hers gentled; his thumbs stroked once across her cheeks. ''Are you okay?''

''Yes, I'm very okay. Thanks for asking.'' She smiled,

and his thumbs caressed the corners of her mouth. She sank into his embrace for a moment before he released her with a rueful shake of his head, scrubbed a hand across his face and muttered something about a big bed and pristine sheets.

"Pardon?"

"I had planned on using a little more finesse. A bed, maybe some foreplay even."

Paris settled in beside him. "Two weeks of foreplay is possibly enough."

"Try six years."

Startled, she sat up straight, only to be hauled back to his side by the arm he threw around her shoulders. "You thought about me for six years?" she asked slowly, while her heart bounded with reckless delight.

"Not every waking moment." He stroked the length of her hair. "But much too often for my peace of mind."

Thinking about her had been an imposition. No doubt he'd fought it with all his incredible willpower. Her heart and her hopes stuttered, but she couldn't stop herself pressing on. "You're making me think I shouldn't have taken your no as a definitive answer."

His hand stilled on her hair, and she felt the weight of his sigh where her head rested between shoulder and chest. "You were just a kid. You didn't know what you wanted."

"I was eighteen, and I knew exactly what I wanted."

"You were having a good time at the party, you were primed for some fun. I was convenient, and you were curious."

"Oh, no, Jack." Paris sat up straight and shook her head adamantly. "I told you before how I felt. It was you I wanted."

"You wanted me so badly that one knock-back sent you running off to London."

"Did you expect I'd hang about, hoping you'd change your mind?"

"No. I didn't expect anything of you, princess." With one finger under her chin, he turned her face toward him and dropped a casual kiss on her forehead. "And I'm trying real hard to make that a habit."

Both his words and his offhand manner stung, but she ducked her head and pretended to smooth out the tails of his shirt so he wouldn't see the hurt reflected in her eyes. From what he'd said earlier, she thought they'd made progress these last weeks, that he would expect something from her. Obviously not.

Take a hint, Paris. Don't expect too much of him.

She brushed her hands down the sides of his shirt and with her best attempt at a casual I-can-handle-this smile, looked up at him. "Well *I* expect something from you."

He went very still.

"I expect you to make good on that brunch you promised."

At first he didn't respond. He watched her with such steady intensity that she started to hope she'd misread him. "That's all you want?" he asked.

Paris's heart pounded. Had she been wrong? Was there an offer for more than food, more than his body, in those fathomless eyes? She reached up, touched his mouth with her fingertips. "I want you," she admitted softly.

And she did—again, already—with a pride-sapping intensity that scared her into pulling away when his lips sought hers. She couldn't do this anymore. Pretending the wanting was purely physical stretched way beyond her acting capabilities.

She scrambled to her feet, needing some distance. "I'm going to take a shower, and then we'll do this brunch thing."

Silence. The weight of his gaze dragged at her, demanding she turn and face him. Wrapping his loose shirt more tightly around her, she lifted one shoulder casually. "That's if you still want to."

"Why wouldn't I?"

Paris didn't know how to respond. Her emotions were way off balance, listing one way and then the other—hardly surprising given the twisting, dipping, soaring roller coaster they'd ridden these past few days.

What did he want from her? A relationship with some kind of strings but involving no expectations. What the heck did that entail? She had to get out of there before she did something desperately uncool and melodramatic, like demanding to know his intentions…or bursting into unprovoked tears.

"I'm taking that shower now," she mumbled, and she was gone before he could answer.

What was that all about?

Jack whipped around the kitchen, opening cupboard doors at random, closing them again when he couldn't recall what he'd been looking for. He scrubbed a hand over his face and leaned back against the counter, forcing himself to be still. The distant hiss of running water permeated the sudden silence, and the heat of frustration permeated his whole body, clawing at him.

Ten seconds, max, and he could be in that bathroom, ripping aside the curtain. Another ten and her wet soap-softened body would be spread against the tiles. With him inside her, demanding the truth. He swore harshly, gripped the edge of the counter.

And what would that prove, Manning?

Nothing that he didn't know already. That one cool shrug of her shoulder as she walked away could turn him into a crazy man. That he couldn't stand any more dewy-eyed declarations of "I want you" without the hows.

How much? In how many ways?

For how long?

He had to know, and he would know…but not in the next minute, and not naked. With a disparaging snort, he acknowledged that skin-to-skin he could demand truths all night long and afterward only remember the exquisite sensation of moving inside her, the savage pleasure of her release closing around him, the joy of his name on her lips, over and over again.

Hell! He gripped the bridge of his nose, squeezed his eyes shut and let out a long whistle of breath. Hell and damn! He had to do something, something other than remember. Coffee. It came to him suddenly, what he'd been searching for. She detested instant, so she must have a machine. He attacked the cupboards more judiciously this time and found what he was looking for behind a plethora of other electrical contraptions.

He smiled with satisfaction, because it was still packaged and came with precise step-by-step instructions. "Things are looking up."

Caffeine underway, he opened the fridge and surveyed its contents. Eggs, no bacon—which eliminated his first choice. He could do pancakes. Midway through a check on the ingredients, he felt the unconscious tensing of his body, and he knew she was there, watching him. Straightening with deliberate care, he reminded himself about handling this patiently. About not letting her undermine his rational purpose.

He turned and found her standing in the doorway, hair spilling around her face, skin all soft and rosy from the shower steam, wearing the palest pink silk wrap and likely nothing else. The impact body-slammed his senses. The only part of his body still functioning hardened instantly...and she looked away, folding her arms defensively.

Jack gave himself a swift mental slap and returned to his task. Several seconds of fruitless searching later, he gave himself a second, harder wake-up call. He'd been searching for flour in the fridge?

"Where do you keep your flour?"

Where was flour usually kept? Paris gave a helpless shrug. Why was he looking for flour?

"You do have some?"

"Well, there are an awful lot of things in the pantry that I never use. Caroline had it stocked for me before I moved in. I guess she thought I cooked."

"Most people do." His reply could have been a casual aside, but the surprise of finding him still here, and her instant response when he turned and fixed her with that sweltering look, had thrown her off balance all over again.

"Maybe I never had anyone to teach me."

He came out of the pantry with a canister and a direct, succinct response. "Maybe you should have enrolled in a course. That's how most people learn a new skill."

She bit her lip, looked away, struggled with the raw prickling at the back of her throat, and called herself all kinds of self-pitying, because he was right. Managed "I'm going to get dressed" before she turned to leave.

"No." Jack barked the order more forcefully than he'd intended, but it worked.

She stopped, straightened her shoulders, and the little movement caused her wrap to shimmer in the fluorescent light, reminding him how it might have been smarter to let her go get more clothes on. But then she turned and lifted that damn chin, and the gaze skittering away from his was the thick wet gray of an overcast sky.

"You won't learn anything if you keep walking away." His voice felt as tight and rough as the knot in his chest. Suddenly he needed something in his hands before he crossed the room and filled them with silk-wrapped woman, before he allowed those big wet eyes to drive all thought of straight talk from his mind. Eat first, straight talk second, bed third, he reminded himself as he went for a low corner cupboard where he'd seen a frying pan earlier.

Bad choice, bending down in jeans, when he'd been imagining his hands in a slow glide over shimmering silk.

Still grimacing, he banged the pan onto the stove and lit a flame under it, opened the utensils drawer and started rummaging. With his focus elsewhere, Paris was able to gather herself. Given a few more minutes, she might even begin to appreciate the sight of Jack moving about her kitchen, seemingly knowing it better than she did.

"What are you making?" she asked.

"Pancakes." He glanced up from the bowl in his hands, stilling her approach with his intense focus. Her breath hitched. Would she ever become used to the effect of that particular look? "What do you like on yours?"

She blinked, nonplussed.

"I think I saw maple syrup in the pantry. You want to get it?"

He turned back to his task. Paris watched, intrigued by the quick, light movement of his hand on the whisk. Big hands, yet so capable and skillful. Her knees wobbled, remembering the skill of his hand on her...and wanting it again so intensely she had to lean against the counter to support herself.

No, she acknowledged, as soon as the initial wave of heat ebbed. *That couldn't satisfy her...not completely. Not anymore.*

"You prefer something else?"

His question cut across her thoughts, caused a mental stumble. How did he know that? She swallowed. "Something else?"

"Other than syrup?" He half turned, went completely still—except for his eyes, instantly hot as they licked all over her—exactly the same as when she first came into the room. And again he turned away abruptly, this time messing about with the pan. "Well?"

Well, what? She backed up on his questions. *You want something else?* Yes. *Other than maple syrup?* Belatedly she realized their cross-purposes.

"I'll get the syrup," she mumbled...if only she knew where to look. "Um...where did you say you saw it?"

"The pantry." He looked decidedly put-out as he tossed the pancake, slammed the pan back onto the stove. "How do you get by without a housekeeper?"

A fair question, Paris told herself, deserving a rational answer. No need to feel it as a slap to her esteem. "I buy things ready-prepared, or I send out."

He tossed the pancake onto a plate and poured more batter without missing a beat. Again it struck her how at home he looked, and she allowed herself a bittersweet moment of longing. Oh, to wake to this every day. Jack, bare-chested and beautiful, in her kitchen...

Bare-chested because his shirt lay in a crumpled heap on her bathroom floor! Cooking because she didn't have a clue!

Hating her uselessness, but determined not to dissolve in another pool of self-pity, she swung across to the pantry. She *would* take lessons. Computer skills *and* cooking. She smiled at her own impetuosity. Perhaps she'd better limit herself to one new skill at a time, starting with the computer stuff she needed for work.

After depositing the syrup next to Jack's growing pancake stack, she searched out cutlery and napkins, and noticed the coffee. He had made real coffee because she hated instant. He was cooking. He had stayed.

"I didn't expect any of this," she said slowly, distinctly, above the joyous upbeat of her heart. "I thought we'd be going out somewhere. No. Actually, I thought you'd be gone."

His hands stilled, but he didn't look up from his cooking. "Would you have preferred that?"

"No. Absolutely not. On both counts." Paused, self-conscious with her admission. "I hope you don't mind doing all the work."

"I don't mind." Revealing nothing, warning her heart not to jump to conclusions. "I like to cook."

"Yes. I can see that." She watched him awhile, appreciating his skill and the rich sweet aroma that curled seductively around her mood, mellowing the edges and teasing her curiosity. "How is it you learned to cook?"

He turned then, lifted one brow quizzically.

"I don't mean to sound sexist, but yours seems like a family with clearly defined men stuff and women stuff. Did *you* do a course?"

A small smile. Better. "No formal course. And you're right about my family. After I left home I had to learn. Self-preservation."

"What, no housekeeper?" she teased.

He laughed out loud, and Paris felt ridiculously gratified. "No hired help. Just four rough bachelors working double shifts. Picture dirty laundry and takeout cartons this high." He gestured waist high with his spatula. "It soon wore thin."

"So my guess is you didn't pick up your kitchen skills from any of those flatmates?"

"From one of their sisters, actually." A small reminiscent smile softened his expression, and Paris's escalating enjoyment flat lined. No. She would not think about what that smile meant, what else he might have learned from his friend's sister. She would not let jealousy ruin her pleasure in sharing this wonderfully light, teasing conversation.

"So when did you move out to Orchard Hills?"

"Almost three years ago."

"Why out there? It's a long drive to work."

"I don't mind the drive. I got sick of apartment living. I needed the space, the air. It's a great family place."

"Yes." She smiled, remembering the rollicking dogs and the kids, but purposefully not thinking about future dogs and kids. "It's just about perfect."

"Just about." His gaze met hers, smile fading as he thought about what he needed to make it absolutely perfect. Her. "There are just a few things I need to take care of first," he added slowly, gravely.

She swallowed, looked uncomfortable, as if she didn't want to hear about those things. And Jack forced himself to take a mental step back. He didn't want to lose this easiness between them. He didn't want her walking away from him again. Not from *him,* he realized with sudden clarity. *From her own feelings.* When she couldn't hide them, she ran from them.

The understanding pleased him, and allowed him to find the right light tone when he turned back to the finished pancakes. "You ready to eat?"

"I thought you'd never ask." She smiled, relaxing visibly as he poured syrup over the first stack. "I hope that plate's mine."

"You couldn't manage half this lot."

"You want to bet? I am *sooooo* famished."

He took the plate to her, cut off a hearty wedge and lifted

it toward her mouth before he noticed her attention had snagged on his chest.

"You have some flour…just there."

"It's not hurting." He directed the fork to her mouth. "Open."

She obeyed. Closed her eyes and moaned melodramatically.

"Good, huh?" He eased closer, close enough to feel the delicate caress of her sleeve against his arm as he lifted the fork again, to smell the light vanilla scent on her skin, to absorb her ambrosial sigh. But no closer.

After another mouthful she pushed his hand away. "You don't have to feed me."

"I don't have to. I want to."

"No one has ever done anything like this for me."

Her simple statement rocked him. Rocked her. He saw the surprise flicker in her eyes, as if she'd thought the words but hadn't meant to say them.

She recovered with a swiftly drawn breath, rushed on. "Themselves, I mean, personally. They've hired someone or sent out. I've had all sorts of things sent out for, but the only people who have ever cooked for me have been paid. Hey, you don't expect to be paid, do you?"

"I don't expect anything."

"You said that before, about not expecting anything."

In the heavy pocket of silence he heard the swish of silk as she shifted her weight, felt it echo somewhere deep inside. A minute shift that brought everything into perfect alignment. Parents who expressed their love with money, a fiancé who'd likely done the same…using her money. No one expecting anything of her, and she giving up on expecting anything from them.

"Yeah, well, I have a confession to make about that." Carefully he slid the plate onto the counter, felt the sudden tension radiating from her body. He backed away a half step and cupped her face between gentle hands. "I lied."

He took a moment's pleasure in the surprised widening of her eyes.

"I do expect things of you—maybe too much. I've been trying to convince myself I expected nothing. Denial. Because the timing is so off." He brushed his lips across her stunned mouth. "The timing is still way off, so how about we start slow, one expectation at a time?"

He touched his thumbs against the corners of her mouth, waited for the slow nod of her head before continuing.

"Let's start with the thing that bothers me most. I hate it when you turn away like you did before, or when I see something flash in your eyes—some thought, some emotion—but you cover it up or push it aside. I want things to be honest between us. I want straight talk. D'you think you can handle that?"

She moistened her lips, eyes focused on his mouth as if watching for the next unexpected word to jump out. "I can try. I want to do that, for you—" She broke off, her voice a little shaky, her eyes worried, and a vague feeling of unease prickled Jack's senses.

"What is it? Is there something you want to get off your chest?"

Her gaze slid away, down, lit on his chest. He felt the beginnings of her smile through the palms of his hands. "There's something on your chest I want to get off."

Then her hand was on him, brushing at the forgotten flour, lingering. Her gaze rose to meet his. "There is something I want to say...but it's so hard to find the words...."

Her voice was no more than a whisper, and as sober as the expression in her stormcloud eyes. Both, and the gentle pressure of her hand where it lay against the heavy pulse of his heart, kindled something immense in Jack. Something that didn't need words. "I know," he murmured, his voice thick with everything he felt. Everything wild and tender, fierce and gentle, simple and complex.

"How is it you know me so well?" she breathed.

"One of life's mysteries."

He bent to taste the slight curl of a smile on her lips, to draw it into his mouth, and as he did, he knew he'd lied again. It was no mystery. It was love.

Twelve

As Jack continued to kiss her with slow doubt-melting thoroughness, all Paris's own expectations imploded in a glittering cascade of images. Jack's perfect home. *Their* puppies and children. Her sisters-in-law calling her rude names across the kitchen sink.

As he carried her to her bed, she felt all kinds of perfect in the gentle strength of his arms, in the possessive way he held her against his heart, in the heady resonance of his pulse under her cheek. Perfect knowledge, perfect rightness, perfect forever.

Together they sank into the softness of her sheets and for a long while—such a long wonderful while—he did nothing but kiss her with that same unhurried giving tenderness, until she felt as if he were drinking from her soul, until she had to pull away before the enormity of love swelling within choked her. And then, only then, did he touch her, first with the warm magic of his gaze and then with those big clever hands, gliding over silk and flesh until she didn't know where one finished and the other began.

"I promised myself slow," he whispered against her neck as he spread her robe. And then the touch of his mouth on her throat, his sweet breath against her aching nipples, the dip of his tongue in her belly button, swamped her in pure-golden sensation. Each new touch felt like the first, alive and glittering with discovery, as if he'd uncovered a new range of senses, as if he could reach past her skin to touch some deeper place. A place she'd never known existed.

She undressed him in a rush, needing to see him, to touch him, to feel him skin to skin, heartbeat to heartbeat. "Slowly," he crooned against her mouth. "Slowly." And then he was kissing her again. Kissing her and kissing her until she settled under the spell of the sensual onslaught. And then he lay perfectly still while she memorized his body, while her palms learned the long, hard planes of his back and her fingertips discovered all the little yielding places, those places that made the breath hiss from his lungs, that made him cry out, "Quit it. That drives me crazy."

And she did quit, because she didn't want him crazy, not even crazy for her. She wanted him absolutely sane and cognizant so he wouldn't miss one of the things she told him with her fingertips and her lips, or with the warmth of her lambent gaze as they lay face-to-face, elevated breaths coiling around them, mingling, entwining, binding them together. Not one of the myriad things she couldn't find words to express.

He slid down her body, the heated glide of his mouth everywhere at once, tormenting her with his thoroughness, too much but never enough, hungry yet restrained, turning her wild and frantic, then soothing her with low, throaty words of restraint and approval. When she felt the strange soft caress of his hair on her inner thighs she trembled with want and need and love. And then the kiss of his tongue— *there!*—shocked the trembling from her body. Until he touched her again, gently, then more boldly, and the delight shivered and shimmered through her body in a quicksilver rush. She fisted her hands in the sheet, clutching for control because this couldn't happen yet, not without him there, inside her, completing her.

Oh, she ached to tell him so, but then he was gone, fumbling through his jeans, protecting himself, and regret stole the words from her lips. Then they were rolling naked, heated skin against skin, stilling with her body beneath his, and he slowly stretched her arms above her head, hands linked and fingers entwined. "Now," he whispered as their gazes connected them. And she opened to him, everything she was and could be, and he buried himself in her body. Deeply, totally, completely.

How had she never known such exquisite pleasure existed? Because it only existed here, in this place, with this one man. With love.

And then he started to move in her, and she tilted her hips and wrapped her legs around him, drawing him deeper to her very center, until the delicious heat was so intense it seared her heart. "Oh, yes," she whispered on a long low exhalation, rocking against him, seeking the bliss that shimmered like a mirage on the rim of her senses. He answered with a guttural plea that was either prayer or entreaty as he moved with long sensuous strokes and a control she felt in the corded muscles of his sweat-slick back. She lifted herself, following the lead of his slow-dance, scoring him with her nails as she tried to gain some purchase on her churning swirling senses.

He groaned, the sound wrenched from deep in his chest,

before he picked up the tempo, building the intensity, filling her with each grinding pulse of his big body, driving them both on until the storm raged around them, picking them up, then tossing them back to earth in wild, tumbling glory.

And she clung to him, replete and complete, because finally she had been able to express how she felt, not in the words her mouth couldn't form, but in loving him with her body and her heart.

The buzz of a phone woke her in the late morning. She tried to ignore it by remembering her earlier wake-up call. A warm hand cruising over her belly, a whispered word against her ear. *Mmmm,* she smiled sleepily, *that had definitely been the perfect awakening.* As opposed to this one....

Face buried in her pillow, she groped for the bedside receiver and dragged it to her ear before her slumberous brain registered the low rumble of a male voice. It wasn't coming from the dead instrument in her hand. She rolled onto her back and focused on the broad set of shoulders rising from the other side of her bed, and then on the cell phone at his ear.

"No problem. The preconstruction estimates went out Friday...."

Paris slumped back into her pillow, his conversation fading as her mind whirled. Sunday morning, and he'd scrambled from her bed to talk business. Obviously he didn't believe in weekends any more than her father did.

The pain she felt wasn't the sharp stab of sudden realization but the solid deep-seated ache of long-time knowledge. She had known from the first night she'd seen him again what kind of man he'd become. She'd watched him work for weeks, seeing his commitment, his single-minded dedication. Knowing he lived for his job. She'd known he wasn't the kind of man she wanted to fall in love with, but she'd gone ahead and done it anyway—not in ignorance, but in stubborn, foolish hope. Despite knowing that men like her father never changed.

The mattress dipped, and she felt his work-roughened hand on her shoulder, then the warmth of his mouth. Her body responded instantly. *It* wanted his mouth to continue. *It* wanted his hands to slide beneath the sheet. Despite the number of times they'd come together in the past twenty-four hours, her body would never have enough. Her body had always been slow to catch up with her brain. And as for her heart... She did not even want to think about her heart.

"You awake?" he murmured from somewhere close by her ear. He'd been so absorbed in his call, he hadn't even heard her fumble with the bedside telephone.

"Why wouldn't I be awake? Unless, of course, you have a silencer on your cell phone."

The hand left her shoulder, and she shivered involuntarily. She felt very cold.

"That was K.G.," he said. "He flew in yesterday."

She turned on her side to find him sitting on the edge of the bed, his back to her. Scratches marred the broad expanse of naked skin, marks of her passion and possession, marks that would fade all too quickly. A strange fear welled in her, an irrational panicky impulse to lay her hands over those marks while they still remained, as if they might fade before her very eyes.

She reached for him, but at the same moment he leaned forward to retrieve his jeans, and her hand dropped back to the sheet.

"He asked us to lunch."

"*Us?*" Paris sat up straight.

He pulled his jeans on before he answered. "I told him I was with you."

Paris closed her eyes. "How did he react to that piece of news?"

"He didn't sound particularly surprised. Said to bring you along."

The mattress moved as he stood. She heard the metallic whirr of his zip. "Bring me, as you'd bring a parcel?"

He grunted, maybe in answer, maybe because he'd gone down below bed level, presumably searching for more clothes.

"Your shirt is in the bathroom."

She opened her eyes as he came back into the room, pushing his arms into his very rumpled shirt. He frowned at the lack of buttons. "I'd forgotten about this." He left it open, sat back on the bed and waited for her unsettled gaze to meet his. "I take it you're not keen on visiting with your father?"

"Right now? With you?" She felt her expression said it all.

A faint smile quirked the corner of his mouth. "We have to face him sometime. Now's as good a time as any."

She looked away, tried to make some sense of her instinctive need to burrow down under the covers and stay put.

He captured her chin and gently turned her to face him. "This is something you have to do, Paris. It's time you stood up to him."

"I do stand up to him."

"Uh-uh. You let him pat you on the head and cut you off midsentence. You'll never earn his respect until you let him know you won't put up with it."

"Will knowing I've spent the past three weeks getting you into my bed earn his respect?"

Paris leaned back against the headboard, effectively re-moving her chin from his hand, but he didn't take the hint. He picked up her hand and linked his fingers with hers. "Showing him you've spent the past three weeks planning a spectacular PR blitz will."

Paris wasn't so sure. Her confidence in her work was too new and fragile to test on her father. And so were her feelings for Jack. Yesterday she'd been so sure, not only when they made love but later, when they talked. Then, wrapped in that brilliant, untarnished cloak of love, she'd been so sure of what she wanted. Today she'd woken to reality, and she needed time to deal with that reality before she made any public proclamations. "I don't want to do this today," she decided.

"You think I do?" He turned her hand over, played with her fingers. A small frown formed between his brows. "He'll try to use this to talk me into staying."

What? Paris shook her head. "Talk you into stay-ing…where?"

"At Grantham's. That's one of the things I wanted to talk to you about." He took her hand to his lips and kissed her fingers. The unexpectedness of the caress curled around her, distracted her for a moment. "We didn't do much talk-ing in the end, did we?"

Oh, they'd talked plenty, but mostly about the past. They'd sidestepped the future very neatly. "When did you make this decision?"

"I always intended leaving, from the day I signed on. I had it all mapped out. Twelve years to absorb everything I could from the best in the game, then I'd have my own business set up before my thirtieth birthday."

Paris did the math. "That was two years ago."

"Yeah. I let K.G. manipulate me into staying longer than I'd intended."

"How did he manage that?"

"By offering me sole management of the Landing Project—my dream job. He knew I couldn't turn it down."

"And when the job's finished, you're free to leave."

"You've got it."

He'll try to use this to talk me into staying. The memory of Jack's words caused a frisson of premonition to goosebump Paris's skin. This was why K.G. had brought her home, why he'd thrown them together. She didn't know how he planned to use their relationship, only that he did.

"Unless K.G. talks you into staying," she suggested slowly.

"Nothing he offers will make a lick of difference."

Paris wished she had Jack's surety. She'd seen her father in bargaining mode too many times to discount his manipulative powers. "You've kept this news under wraps. I haven't heard any mention of it around the office. Your sisters didn't mention it the other night."

"Only K.G. and my own personal staff know my plans. I didn't want it that way, but K.G. insisted."

"And when K.G. insists…" She couldn't keep the bitter edge out of her voice. His grip on her fingers tightened in perfect painful counterpoint, forcing her eyes back to his.

"It isn't like that. I need his good word when I leave. It can make or break my business."

Of course. His own business. He had mentioned that earlier. "You didn't consider joining Mannings'?"

He looked as though the very thought horrified him. "They impose enough on my private life. I couldn't work with them, too. Why did you ask?"

"I just thought, seeing as you're in the same business…" Her voice trailed off.

"I started out there, when I left school, back when there was only Dad and me. But before I even finished my apprenticeship, we'd logged about a hundred fights. We couldn't work together, you know.''

Paris didn't know. She'd never had a stand-up fight with her father, not because she'd never wanted to, but because she'd never had the nerve. Or maybe because he'd never felt anything in her life was important enough to fight over. ''What did you argue about?''

''Direction. Expansion. Dad was a builder, and that was it. He didn't have any aspirations beyond building good houses.''

''And along came Jack with aspirations.''

''I figured anyone could build houses. I wanted to build landmarks.''

''Past tense?''

''Hell, no! But I sure don't want to build any more apartment towers. The Landing was different. It inspired me to look at different options. I want to do the same thing on a lesser scale in the suburbs.''

Paris heard the excitement in his voice, saw the enthusiasm alight in his eyes. She struggled to her feet, dragging the tangled sheet with her. She didn't want to hear about his ambitions, the future he'd mapped out, all constructed around work.

''Hey, what's up?'' he called to her retreating back.

''Have to use the bathroom,'' she muttered, and she kept on walking.

''Hang on just a minute.'' Paris didn't hang on, but he caught her just inside the bathroom, swung her around to face him. ''If there's something on your mind, something I've said to upset you, spit it out.''

''It's nothing. Forget it.''

''We made an agreement. Honesty, remember?'' She tried to spin away, but he transferred his hold from the sheet to her upper arms, holding her in place, trapped between his bulk and the bathroom door, trapped by the questions in his eyes. "Is it because I'm leaving Grantham's?"

"Oh, it's that and everything." To her consternation, she felt her eyes start to fill with tears, and that wasn't what she wanted at all. She wanted to be strong and cool and together. She settled for honest. "It's because what you said reminded me so much of someone else I know."

"Who?" He stared back at her, utterly clueless, and she laughed harshly, a short sharp burst of air.

"Only my father!"

"You think I'm like your father? You think I'm another K.G.?" He struggled with his astonishment, then shook his head and let her go so abruptly she almost fell. "When did you arrive at this brilliant deduction?"

Paris hauled the sheet higher and lifted her chin. "Have you ever heard his life story?" she asked. "How he got started in this business?"

"I haven't had the privilege."

"You don't need to hear it. You just repeated it."

He leaned back against the basin, eyes narrowed.

"Bright youth full of ambitious zeal fights with father, then heads off at a million miles an hour to conquer the world of construction. He makes his mark well before he hits thirty, but you know what? There's always another mark. Another goal. Another point to prove to himself and to the world in general."

"That's not the way it is. Not with me."

"No?" Paris hauled the sheet up higher. "Do you want to hear the rest of the story? The part about his family? He has a wife and a daughter—only one daughter, you understand, because he isn't home long enough for any more. There's always a project more important, a deal more urgent, a meeting he can't miss. Before he knows it, his wife's gone, his daughter's all grown-up, and you know what the saddest part is?''

A muscle worked in his jaw.

"He doesn't *know* his daughter. He must love her—everybody says so—because he buys her everything he thinks she wants. But hey, he has money to burn, so he can afford it.'' She paused, needed to swallow, to ease the constriction in her throat. "He probably does love her, but he knows nothing about her, how she thinks, what she's really like—'' she pressed a hand to her chest for emphasis, and to ease the hurt ''—inside where it matters!''

"You think I don't know all this?'' He pushed himself away from the basin and closed his hands around the tops of her arms. Hunched down to look into her face. "I was there, remember?''

Paris backed away so his hands dropped from her arms. She didn't want him touching her, talking to her in that low intense voice. Talking her into believing him.

"I know what you missed out on, Paris. I can give you those things. I can give you what you want.''

Could he? Did he really know what it would take to fill those lonely recesses of her soul? Oh, it would be so easy to believe him. Then to sit at home waiting for him at the end of fourteen-hour days, to grow greedy for his time, needy for his company. To listen to excuses. *Next year it'll be easier. When this project's finished I'll have more time.* To grow tired of the excuses, to turn cold and brittle like her mother.

She rubbed her arms to ward off the chill, and her grip on the sheet loosened. It slumped low over her breasts before she reclaimed it. His gaze tracked the movement involuntarily—and he regretted it. She saw the annoyance as he recovered abruptly, his expression tight.

Paris smiled and hoped it didn't look as stiff and fake as

it felt. She let the sheet drop all the way to the floor. "Yes, Jack. You can give me *exactly* what I want."

His jaw tensed. "That's not what I meant, and you know it."

Paris looked at him through her lashes. Sultry-and-steamy she could try for. What-she-really-needed and what-Jack-could-make-up-for she wouldn't take risks on. So when she stepped around him to reach for the shower taps, she deliberately didn't step wide enough. She let her hip brush by his, linger a moment.

"I think I need a shower," she said. Hot water gushed into the cubicle, clouding the room with steam. She adjusted the temperature and stepped under the spray.

Jack took a giant mental leap away from her naked curves, the invitation in her eyes, the provocative pout of her lips. He fixed on a spot on the tiles just beyond her right ear and shook his head. "No, princess. That's not what you need from me."

"But it's what I want from you. It's all I want from you."

Jack shifted his gaze a few inches to the left. He could barely see her eyes through the steam, so he moved closer. "Uh-uh, that's a lie, and we both know it."

He felt very strong, strong enough to lean right into the shower, to place his hands on the wet tiles on either side of her head. To allow the heavy spray to saturate his head and shoulders and shirt, to kiss her hard on her startled mouth. He leaned back a few inches and looked right into her blinking eyes.

"I'm not your father. I'm a man who enjoys his job, who probably works too hard, too many hours, but only because I take my responsibilities seriously. I take all my responsibilities seriously, at work and at home."

He paused, let that sink in. "Yesterday, after that first

time when I lost it, you said you trusted my sense of responsibility. That trust blew me away, Paris, and I don't think it was empty rhetoric. I know it wasn't empty rhetoric—I saw it in your eyes.'' He backed off a little, asked quietly, ''What happened to that trust?''

He saw the stunned expression in her eyes, watched her throat work, and knew she couldn't answer. Knew he couldn't stand firm if she started to cry.

''I'm going to take my shower at the office, not because I love the place so much I can't stay away, but because I know I have a shirt stashed there—a dry one, with buttons.'' He grabbed a towel from the rack and scrubbed at his head. ''Then I'm going to see K.G., and I'll listen to whatever he throws my way, which I suspect is going to be you, or some package including you. I'll listen, and I'll try to contain my anger, and I'll politely say 'No, thanks,' not because I don't want you in every conceivable way, but because I won't see him use you.

''I want you to be there, Paris, because this concerns you as much as me. My future concerns you. Think about that, and think about taking a stand against your father so he doesn't keep on using you.''

He kissed her hard on the lips.

''One more expectation. There'll be no more talk about wanting only sex from me. We've gone way past that point. Let there be no misunderstanding about that.''

Thirteen

Wait! No! Hang on! If she could only get her mouth to function, she could voice the words screaming from her brain. If she could only get her jelly-legs to cooperate, she would be out that door and chasing him down the corridor, stark-staring naked. But she wouldn't care, probably wouldn't even notice.

Jack wanted her in his future. He wanted her.

How could she love him so much and misjudge him so severely? How could she love him so much and be too afraid to say the words? She clambered from the shower and swiped the mirror clean with her forearm. Leaned close, looked right into her own eyes and spoke straight and honest.

"You're right, Jack, this isn't about sex."

"I don't want you only for sex. That was a lie."

"I love you."

Rocked back with a small smile of accomplishment playing around her mouth. ''There—that wasn't so difficult, was it?''

But then the mirror misted over until all she could see was a vague impression of her face, and a nebulous shadow of doubt settled over her. She swung away, toweling herself dry as she strode into her bedroom, scrubbing at her skin with a vigor she hoped would erase this strange sense of…unease. She frowned. No, not purely unease. There was also an element of urgency, a need to find Jack and spill those words before she lost her courage. Before her father interceded.

She snatched underwear from her dresser, but her clumsy hands fumbled and shook. Getting all her limbs into the right holes took a supreme effort. She took a deep, calming breath, let it go.

And as she rifled through her hangers, she decided a little help with staying cool wouldn't hurt. She flicked straight past the bright reds—she would need no help with mad raving rage once K.G. started patting her on the head. She rejected anything frivolous or frothy—she would have no trouble with dithering incoherence when she tried telling Jack how she felt about him.

At the very end of the rack she found it. A classic shift in serene porcelain-blue, a gift from her mother and never worn. She slipped it over her head, felt it settle against her skin like a cool breeze, and she prayed its effect might miraculously seep through her pores. She rolled stockings onto her legs with impatient hands, swore in a most unserene manner when her loose bracelet-watch caught and snagged. Found another pair, took a deep breath and tried again, more carefully. Tied her hair at the back of her neck with a silk scarf, slipped her feet into matching pumps, and was out the door before her nerve deserted her.

* * *

When Jack powered his Explorer between the ornate pillars marking the entrance to K.G.'s harborside estate and saw the car already sitting at the top of the drive, his right foot eased reflexively. She'd taken a lot less thinking time than he'd imagined.

"What are you doing here?" he muttered as he pulled up alongside the low-slung sports car. It offered no comment.

Jack killed his engine and frowned down at the mute Porsche. Maybe she hadn't needed any thinking time at all. Maybe she'd simply needed to talk to her father. Maybe she'd hared straight over here to tackle him head on. Maybe she'd sent the car home with a message telling K.G. exactly where he could stick all future offers of help.

Irritated with himself and the extent of his pointless *maybe*ing, he jumped down from his vehicle and slammed the door. More logical to get himself inside and find out the reason. As he scrunched across the gravel drive to the front entrance, the midday sun shone unimpeded from a cloudless sky, warming the shirt on his back, but as he stepped into the shaded portico, a sudden chill touched him like an icy tentacle of foreboding. He lifted a hand to the bell and snorted in disgust.

"Foreboding, my—"

The door swung open to reveal a glowingly tanned Caroline. "Jack, darling!" she enthused, and he was immediately enfolded in a flurry of air kisses and expensive French perfume. "We are so glad you could come."

Caroline linked arms and propelled him toward the conservatory. It was a long walk, but Caroline had more than enough small talk to last the distance. All Jack had to do was smile and make appropriate noises of assent until she declared, "Here we are, then."

At first he thought the room was empty. Outside the

French windows, K.G. paced the terrace, a phone at his ear. Then Jack saw a flicker of movement to his left, and Caroline said, "Aaah, there you are, Paris. I found this gorgeous man lurking on the front steps. Do you think we should keep him?"

Paris occupied a cane easy chair, a long glass in her hand, too far away for him to get a handle on her mood.

"I'm considering it," she said carefully.

"Oh, good," Caroline said with a laugh, oblivious to the undercurrents ripping across the room. "Then I'd best get him a drink. What would you like, Jack?"

"A light beer," his voice told Caroline, but his eyes fixed on Paris. *I would like to know what you're considering,* those eyes told her.

Caroline's heels clacked a staccato rhythm across the Italian-slate floor. "Any preference?" she called gaily. "I think I can rustle up a nice Belgian brew."

"Perfect." *Especially if you have to go to Belgium to fetch it.*

Aware they had little time alone, he started across the big room, slowing when he saw how cool she looked.

"So. You did decide to come—"

"I thought you'd never get here—"

They both spoke at once, both stopped at the same time, eyes connecting, questioning.

"If I'd known you would change your mind so quickly, I'd have waited and brought you myself," he said.

"Well, that's me, always making up my mind too quickly, then changing it again."

"Only about coming here?" Jack asked carefully, as he took the seat next to hers.

"No. I have changed my mind a great many times these past few weeks." She paused to moisten her lips and smooth her already smooth skirt. Worried eyes met his, slid away. "I know you asked me to speak straight, but I'm finding it very difficult."

She uncrossed her legs with a slither of silk. Recrossed them. A nail tapped the side of the glass. Not as cool as Jack had thought.

"When you left, right after you left, I knew exactly what I had to say to you, and I knew I had to say it fast, because once my father starts…well, I know what he's going to say, and I absolutely know you won't like it. I'm afraid it will change the way things are, have been." The words tumbled from her in an airy rush, then cut off abruptly. She drew a deep shuddery breath and whispered, "I'm sorry…that's not it at all."

I know what he's going to say.

That same wintry chill he'd felt earlier tracked a slow path up his spine. *What did she know? And why was she apologizing?*

"That's not what I wanted to say to you. I wanted to tell you how I feel…about you." Her whisper-soft voice and the even softer look in her eyes eased over Jack, chasing away his concerns. He reached across and took her fidgety hands in his.

"How *do* you feel about me?"

He lifted her hands to his lips and pressed a kiss to each. Registered the soft drawing of breath, the brush of her knees against his, someone clearing their throat. It wasn't Paris.

He looked up to find Caroline and K.G. watching them, Caroline's brilliant blue eyes agog with curiosity, approval radiating from K.G.'s tanned face.

"Well, Caro, it seems this pair did stop bickering while we were away. I told you throwing them together would do the trick."

Jack felt Paris's knee-jerk reaction, and he gripped her

fingers tighter so they wouldn't slip free. "Giving her the Landing PR job was your best trick," he said calmly, distinctly. "Congratulations. Your judgment was spot-on."

"No need to congratulate me. Just thank me for bringing my daughter home for you."

"Thank you," he said obligingly. "I'm confident Paris's work will make the difference with the Landing."

K.G. dismissed that with a casual wave of his whisky glass. "You know I'm not talking about work. I'm talking about you two, together."

"Really, Kevin!" Caroline reprimanded. "You're embarrassing poor Paris."

"I don't have time to beat around the bush, not when he's got this damn fool idea about leaving Grantham's."

"I *am* leaving."

K.G. grunted his disgust. "You've got rocks in your head. You play your cards right, you have a ready-made business without going anywhere."

"That's not something I'm interested in. I suggest you go no further down that path."

Jack sounded even, controlled, calm...all the things Paris wasn't, and not only because they were talking around her, as if making that scarcely veiled reference to Grantham's succession didn't involve her. As if *she* wasn't the card K.G. referred to.

"Why don't you go see to some lunch, Caro?" K.G. suggested.

"Now that's a good idea. Would you like to help me, Paris?"

"Actually, I would rather speak with my father. Perhaps Jack can help you. He's much more use in a kitchen than I am."

In the moment of silence before Caroline's laughter tinkled across K.G.'s blustering, Paris felt the reassuring squeeze of Jack's hand. "My pleasure." He smiled at Caroline, then he leaned across to press a solid, inspiring kiss to Paris's lips and murmured, "Don't wimp out."

K.G. watched him leave through narrowed eyes, then whipped around to face Paris, grudging, annoyed. "All right, princess, you have my attention. What is it you have to say?"

Oh, she had so much to say, she didn't know where to start. Probably she should start with the thing eating at her most. "When you rang me in London, when you told me you had a special project for me, what project did you have in mind?"

"Milson Landing, what else?"

Paris snorted. "Don't treat me like a fool, Daddy. You have just admitted to bringing me home in the hope Jack and I would get together. What I want to know is why?"

"Seems to me you should be thanking me, not asking all these damn fool questions."

Paris shook her head, steadied her rising anger, took another tack. "What gave you the idea that we should be together, when we hadn't seen each other in six years?"

He watched her for a moment through narrowed eyes, then hitched one shoulder in a why-not-tell-her? gesture. "I remember the way you used to follow him about all those years ago, knew you had a crush on him. I didn't mind— it was half the reason I invited him around. Heard about you throwing yourself at him at that party, too, but you were too young and headstrong back then to know what you wanted. Getting mixed up with that twit over in London proved that."

He stopped to refill his glass without offering to do the same for Paris. She didn't care. Alcohol would be no help for the sick churning in her stomach.

"All the time you were away, neither of you missed an

opportunity to ask about the other, so when Jack started pestering me about getting someone for this job and you were over there at loose ends, I figured I'd do you both a favor.''

"You want me to believe you did this for our benefit? Since when did you do anything for anyone's benefit except your own?''

K.G. looked genuinely shocked. ''That's not true, princess. I've always done everything for you.''

Paris's reply was a strangled mixture of incredulous laughter and pain.

''I don't see what you're in such a state about. You've never complained before.''

''Believe me, I was complaining on the inside!'' She slapped a hand to her heart. ''In here I was complaining. You never looked deep enough, Daddy. You never looked beyond the surface.''

''You're so unhappy?''

''Yes. No.'' She threw her hands in the air. ''I was happy doing this job. I've never been happier, thinking that finally I was doing something of use, that I might earn some respect. Make you proud.''

''I'm proud of you, princess.''

''And you show it by bringing me home with some ridiculous idea of using me as an incentive to keep Jack on at Grantham's?''

''Now hang on a minute, princess—''

''No, I won't hang on while you patronize me with more of this rubbish about being proud of me and doing me a favor. You let me believe you wanted me home to work with you, when all the time you were cooking up some scheme.'' She stopped abruptly, needed to pull herself together, because the tears were threatening. ''That's the bit I don't get. How is it you expect me to prevent Jack leaving

Grantham's? What influence do you possibly think I can have over him?''

At least he had the grace to look uncomfortable. But maybe that was only the threat of her tears. K.G. had never been comfortable with tears.

''You threw us together based on my teenage crush and a few casual inquiries. You left us together for three weeks, and you come back expecting…what? Wedding plans?''

She'd meant it as a joke, but the joke was on her. She laughed, incredulous, at the expression on K.G.'s face.

''You're serious, aren't you? You seriously expected…?'' She couldn't finish the sentence. Could only shake her head. ''That's a little presumptuous even for you, Daddy.''

''I didn't presume. I hoped.''

Paris saw the mulish set to his shoulders, knew she would get no truths from him easily. Tried to think as he would think. ''Jack was aiming to leave, and you were running out of options. You figured there might be an attraction between us, threw us together, hoped we'd fall in love. Then, as your prospective son-in-law, you could offer him the business and he'd stay.''

His silence was answer enough.

Paris laughed, shook her head. ''That is so far-fetched.'' And the more she thought about the implausibility, the more she laughed, and the more she laughed, the more she realized how much she'd wanted exactly that to happen. The instant falling in love, the wedding plans. Everything.

''We can talk him into staying.''

''You and me and which army?'' She brought her mirth under control, realizing that there had been a touch of hysteria to it. ''I don't have that kind of influence, Dad. Honestly. What we have is not some whirlwind romance. There will be no wedding.''

But K.G. wasn't prepared to settle for that. She could see the bullheaded determination in his eyes, and it sparked her temper—not to a hot, raging anger but to a cool strong purpose. She needed to know how far he would go, how far he would pursue this before he let it be.

"Do you want me to plead your case, Daddy? Or, hey, I could ask him to marry me. What should I offer him first up? A seat on the board of directors would have to be a minimum."

"I have Legal working on a contract."

Of course he would. "Is there a prenuptial? I think there should be a prenuptial. Grantham executives have a notoriously high divorce rate."

"Don't get sassy with me, girl."

"I'm not being sassy. I am being calm and reasonable about this. If you want me to talk Jack into staying and marrying me, it is only fair we cover all the contingencies."

She swung away and came up short, eyes widening in shock.

"Jack! How long have you been standing there?"

"Long enough." He came a little further into the room, and Paris noted the firm set of his lips, the masked expression. "I didn't mean to eavesdrop. Caroline sent me to fetch you for lunch. In the green room. I won't be staying."

"What—there's a problem? Which site?" K.G. asked.

"It's not a site problem, it's personal." Jack's eyes flicked in Paris's direction. "Nothing I shouldn't have worked out for myself." Flicked back to K.G.. "Caroline said you should go through. Would you mind passing on my apology?"

The sick churning in Paris's stomach intensified. What had she said? What could have brought that cold bleak look to Jack's face?

"I think you've misconstrued what you just heard."

"I think I misconstrued plenty of things this weekend."

"Oh, Jack, let me explain." She started toward him, but he stopped her with a look.

"Save it, Paris. I'm not in the mood for explanations."

He wouldn't be in the mood for a long, long while. The chill that had been walking all over his body had settled in the pit of his stomach the moment she turned and the initial surprise turned to guilt, then melted beneath that cool smile. That deceptive mask.

"You asked me to speak straight, don't you think you should do the same?"

"Straight talk." Jack dismissed the notion with a slash of his hand. "What was it you were trying to tell me earlier? Were you trying to warn me? To confess you'd been part of this deceit all along?"

"No." She lifted her chin, looked him right in the eye. "Actually, I wanted to tell you that I love you."

Jack felt each word like a punch—right in the tight knot she'd twisted him in from the very start. He wanted to believe her, wanted to see past the pain to what might be…but he couldn't. "I might have believed that if I'd heard it earlier."

"And you might not have." She seemed to withdraw, to pull everything that had shone in her eyes back within. "I'm sorry you can't see past your preconceptions of who I am. I'm sorry you can't see past my surname."

"Believe me, I'm sorry, too."

Fourteen

Somehow Paris managed to drag herself through the four weeks leading up to the Milson Landing launch, courtesy of what she'd learned from Jack. Last thing every night, she made to-do lists and scheduled her next day item by item. She refused to think of what would happen afterward, when she didn't have all her lists and plans and schedules to keep her going, one step after another.

Refusing to think about Jack was pointless. A hundred times she'd thought to ring him, but what would she say? What could she say to the man she loved who thought so poorly of her?

She saw him a total of three times, twice mere glimpses, the third when she came across him without warning, walking through the lobby with that loose-hipped stride, his suit coat slung over his shoulder and held there by a fingertip. The impact knocked her sideways, drove the air from her lungs, leaving her aching and breathless, as if she'd run headlong into a solid wall of heartache.

What would it have been like if he'd noticed her? If she'd had to endure some polite conversation? No, she definitely was not up to that, so she moved about the office with great care, avoiding any chance encounters.

And after two more weeks he would be gone for good. No more chance sightings. No more Jack.

Four weeks had proved a tight time frame, but with her meticulous planning, she'd managed to pull it together. The Landing launch looked as though it would be a huge success. Five hundred and ten of the *mega* megarich were schmoozing in the deepening twilight of the Milson Landing gardens. The Heart of Gold Committee would make a very tidy profit, while she exposed the For Sale signs to some very tidy bank balances. She had done the work, she had got them here, the rich and the media, and now she was relying on the Landing to weave its magic.

For the very first time it had no effect on Paris. Her listless eyes scanned the growing throng and she didn't feel a thing. No pride in her work. No sense of accomplishment. Nothing but an immense overpowering sadness because she'd thought this would mean so much to her and it didn't. It was just a job after all.

Jack scowled into his untouched glass of champagne, shook his head, tried to concentrate on the conversation flowing around him.

"...Kidman's joking if he thinks I'll buy the quantity over plan..."

"...the load-bearing walls gave way and down she came..."

"...not slate, need something showier..."

His kind of people talking his kind of talk. It was boring the pants off him. He glanced away, caught the glitter of raspberry sequins and a flash of honey-colored hair through the crowd. His chest felt unbearably tight. Then the crowd parted for a moment, long enough for him to spot her companion. K.G. was puffed up with pride and satisfaction, but for once Jack didn't feel any of the bitter anger. All he felt was deep wrenching pain.

He had to get out of here. He didn't know why he'd bothered to come, only that he couldn't stay away. This time he wouldn't give in to the urge to wade through the sea of dinner suits and designer dresses, to grab her by the shoulders and shake her. To remind her how it had been between them and how it should be.

She didn't want a future; she'd made that perfectly clear. He could still hear her voice, clear and calm and final. *There will be no wedding.* And wasn't that the killer? Jack did. Nothing less would do.

He turned sharply, shouldered his way through the crowd, found leaving wasn't so easy. Too many people wanted to shake his hand, to talk business. Wasn't this what he'd wanted? Wasn't this exactly why he'd stayed on at Grantham's those extra years? To make use of this night, these accolades, to promote his own business?

The simple fact was that he couldn't bring himself to care anymore. He excused himself again, had almost cleared the perimeter of the party when the microphone crackled to life, then squealed in protest at some heavy-handed punishment. The group near him closed ranks, blocking his exit. Resigned, he faced the stage. What did another half hour matter? It wasn't as if he had anywhere else to be.

Paris looked up toward the stage recently vacated by a rather fine jazz band. She blanched when she saw K.G., aglow with a combination of fine scotch whisky and pride in the success of the evening. Her fingers grasped at Caroline's arm.

"I said no speeches," she hissed.

"I'd say there's precious little you can do about it." Caroline said with a smile, holding Paris back. "Except cringe and bear it."

Caroline was right. There was nothing she could do without making a scene, and K.G. full of blown-up pride was a far better prospect than a K.G. belligerent because she'd tried to stop him. "Is this thing working?" he boomed into the microphone.

A ripple of laughter, the turning of heads, the drop in conversation, informed him it was.

"Are you all having a good time?"

"We're enjoying your Bolly, K.G.," one loud voice informed him.

"Well good for you, and good for me." Laughter. "But there's someone else you should thank for the champagne and everything else you're enjoying this evening. Where are you, Paris?" He peered into the crowd.

"Over here, K.G.," yelled a voice in front of her, and suddenly it seemed like five hundred heads had turned her way.

She mouthed a fervent but ineffectual *No* back at the stage. K.G. was too far away to read it. "I expressly said no speeches," she mumbled at Caroline.

"It doesn't look like she's coming up here. Never known a Grantham to be shy."

More laughter.

K.G. waited for it to die down, his expression now serious, eyes fixed on Paris. "This affair is my daughter's doing, all hers. Her conception, her effort, her hard work."

Applause.

"And I want her to know in front of all you witnesses, that I couldn't be more proud of her. She seems to have this damn fool idea about going to college and doing some course and, being my daughter, she's proving stubborn. I can't seem to change her mind, so I'd very much appreciate it if any of you freeloaders can talk some sense into her. But if you all fail...Paris, you know there's always a job for you here. Any time you want it."

More applause, but it was only a dull noise in Paris's ears. Was it possible for tears to blur one's hearing as well as vision?

Her father was looking right at her, his voice dropping as if he was speaking to her alone. "I have it on good authority that I don't say this often enough. I love you, Paris."

And it didn't matter that five hundred party guests, hundreds of them total strangers, shared this moment. It only mattered that he'd said the words.

Paris picked her way through the crowd, which, microphone turned off, quickly lost interest. No one took much notice when she finally made it to the stage and threw her arms around her father's neck. "I love you, too, Daddy," she whispered through the tears. "But I'm not changing my damn fool stubborn mind. It's totally made up on this one."

He hugged her tightly, then put her aside. "You going to do something about that other thing that's fixed in your damn fool stubborn mind?"

She didn't even bother asking. "What can I do?"

"You've become pretty good at speaking your mind lately, but I suggest you could use some more practice." He smiled, and Paris swore she saw a sheen of moisture in his eyes. "Go on, before I get the two of you and bash your heads together. He's over there near the big—"

"I know where he is." She leaned up and planted a kiss on her father's cheek. "Thank you, Daddy."

He was leaving. As she excused her way through the crowd and cursed the narrow skirt and high heels that slowed her progress, she could see him shaking hands with several men, a hand lifted in farewell, and she felt a huge panicky fear. Then overwhelming relief when she pushed through the last cluster of people and saw his dark figure striding away.

"Jack."

He stopped, whipped around, and she felt his eyes sharply focused on hers. Her mouth turned dry from the impact. Her heart hammered against her ribs. She had no idea what she was going to say, only that she had to say something. She almost ran the last ten yards to catch him, and then she simply stood there staring idiotically. He looked so big and right and solid and *there,* and all she wanted to do was walk right up and rub her face against that warm broad chest. "You're leaving?"

He cut a glance to the car park to his right. "Seems like."

Awkwardness closed around her with the gathering darkness. She looked away. "I wasn't sure you'd come."

"I had to." She felt the intensity of that gaze again, drawing her eyes back to his.

"Yes, well, it's yours. Of course you had to."

He said nothing, just watched her, and in the deep harsh shadows he looked hard, mouth set, expression closed. And it felt to Paris as if her heart had jammed itself in her throat, blocking the words she wanted to say. She looked past his shoulder, hoped the words might mysteriously appear on the wall of the nearest villa, like some providential cue card. The words to let him know how wrong she'd been.

Words of trust and love. True to form there was nothing on the wall but ivory paint, and she knew she wasn't going to be getting her help from outside. It would have to come from inside.

"Congratulations on tonight," he said finally, breaking the long stretch of silence. "It's a serious success."

"Thank you. Not just for the sentiment—" which could have come from anyone and didn't mean a thing "—but for making this possible. I wouldn't be here if it weren't for you."

"Oh, I think you'd have gotten along—"

"No," she said, overriding that detestably polite tone. "I shouldn't have been given the job, we both know that, but you spent a lot of time with me. You taught me a great deal."

"You were a quick teach." A pause. "So, are you really going to college?"

"That's my plan. A marketing degree. But that's next year, so I have a few months to fill between now and then."

"I'm sure K.G. will find you something to work on."

She shook her head. "Do you really think I could continue to work with my father?"

"You seem to be getting along fine."

"We're getting along *better,* but that doesn't mean I've forgotten or forgiven what he did, or that I'd trust him again. He used me, Jack, as much as you think I was using you."

He moved, seemed to shrug something off. A hand went to the back of his neck, rubbing. "I have to be going."

"Still working nights?" She bit her lip. "I'm sorry. That was uncalled for."

"No, that was legitimate. We both know I worked too hard. And to answer your question, no, I'm not working nights."

"How is your business going?"

"I haven't done much in that direction yet."

"Why ever not?"

"I'm taking a little break, reassessing."

"I can't imagine you kicking back." She took a closer look at his face, at the tired eyes, and knew he hadn't been kicking back enough. "Have you been away?"

"No. I've been working on Mum's house."

"How's that going?" She hated this stilted chitchat, but worse, she hated the idea of it stopping, of him walking away.

"She moved in Wednesday."

"I hope she likes it." So polite, so not-what-she-wanted-to-say.

She heard the shift of his weight, saw the small hitch of one shoulder, and she knew he was about to go. *No.* She dredged deep for some courage. Everything positive that had happened these past months had happened because she made an effort. Tonight hadn't come about because her father had given her a job; tonight had come about because she'd worked hard at that job. Her relationship with K.G. hadn't changed by chance; it had changed because she'd made him sit up and take notice.

So was she going to stand here while the most important thing in her life walked away? Or was she going to make an effort?

She took a step closer, felt her heel catch between pavers, and she teetered, felt the steadying strength of his hands on her shoulders. "You all right?"

"Not really."

"I suppose you're wearing those spiky heels again."

"Yes, but that's not the problem." Deep breath, ignore the giddying scent of his nearness. "I didn't get that thank-you right. I have to do a better job of it. You gave me this—tonight—but that's not what matters. You gave me a shot at a better relationship with my father, and that *is* important, but not as important as what you gave me here, in my heart. You gave me confidence and strength and courage to believe in myself, to start making my own choices. That's what I have to thank you for."

And with courage beating hard in her chest, she stepped closer, reached up and kissed his cheek. Felt his absolute stillness. "I don't want your polite little thank-you kisses. If you're going to be confident and strong, at least have the courage to kiss me properly."

"I can't do that." Her voice sounded breathy and reedy, not like the strong woman she'd wanted to be.

"Why not? Spit it out, Paris."

"I'm not that strong. I can't kiss you and pretend nothing happened between us. I love you too much to pretend anymore."

There. She'd said it, and apart from the aching tightness like a vise around her chest, it hadn't hurt a bit. Bolstered, she continued, had to explain, to get it all out there.

"You didn't believe me that day, and that hurt more than you can imagine, that lack of faith. When I said I knew my father's intentions, I meant instinctively. Not because we'd planned it together. And I figured if you loved me, you'd know me well enough to know that."

"What about the no wedding? Did you mean that, too?"

Paris stared at him, hardly daring to believe, to listen to her heart's leap of hope. Then a departing car swung their way, and they were caught in the bright arc of headlights, and what Paris saw on his face, in those beautiful eyes, flooded her heart.

"I would consider a wedding, very seriously, should the question ever arise."

He laughed softly, a husky joyous sound that she tasted

on his lips as he bent to kiss her, hungrily, as if he would never stop. As if he'd missed her as much as she'd missed him—a kiss that took possession of her mouth and everything she was, until all she knew was Jack. Then he pulled her close against the escalated beat of his heart, hands big and warm and strong against her bare back.

"Just stay there, don't move," he breathed against her hair. "If you don't move and I don't look into your eyes, I might be able to say what I have to say."

"You don't have to explain."

"Yes, I do. These past weeks, I've had time to do a lot of thinking about what matters and what doesn't matter. I thought business, my job, mattered as much as anything to me, but I was wrong. It meant nothing when I thought I had lost you. Nothing is worth that.

"I've been making some plans." He laughed dryly; she felt the slight shake of his head. "I'm trying to give them up, but old habits die hard. Lew has agreed to come on with me, and that'll ease the pressure, means I won't have to work sixteen-hour days. Not every day.

"I thought a lot about what you said about your parents, and I would never do that to you. Never."

"I know that." She smiled against the reassuring strength of that big, warm chest. "I've been thinking, too. I know you're not my father, but I also know I'm not my mother. I would never let you get away with that. I would not sit at home and put up with it."

"I know." He eased her away a little, held her so he could look into her face. "I do know you, sweetheart, and I believe everything you said before. God, I have missed you so much. It's been like my heart's been cut out. How is it that I came to love you so much so fast?"

She pressed a kiss to his throat, too choked with happiness for words.

Then he stilled suddenly, cursed. "All this talk about work and I haven't said the most important things. I need to listen to my own advice about straight talk."

And then he was looking right into her eyes with that serious, intent look that floored her every time. No. She would never become immune to that particular look, nor to the words he was speaking, "I love you, Paris. Marry me. Be my wife, my friend, my partner."

Straight talk in short sentences, but every one of them large enough to wrap itself around Paris's heart. She looked right into Jack's eloquent eyes, eyes that spoke of his love and his knowledge of her love.

"I love you, too, so much that sometimes I can scarcely bear it." She rose on her toes and pressed a kiss to his lips. "Yes. I will marry you."

A broad grin spread across Jack's mouth. He wrapped his arms around her back, lifted her and whirled her around until she squealed out loud. "Stop, stop!"

He spun her to a stop and slid her very slowly down his body. The combination of body contact and spinning left her giddy.

"I take it those were the correct answers?" she said.

And with that he bent and picked her up, tossed her over his shoulder.

Paris lost her breath and her bearings. "What are you doing? Where are you taking me?" Upside down, it was impossible to tell anything except that they were moving. Fast.

She sighed blissfully again.

It didn't matter which direction they headed, she knew exactly where he was taking her. He was taking her home.

* * * * *

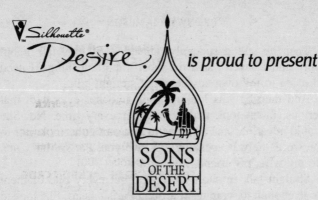

SILHOUETTE® MAKES YOU A STAR!

Feel like a star with Silhouette.

We will fly you and a guest to New York City for an exciting weekend stay at a glamorous 5-star hotel. Experience a refreshing day at one of New York's trendiest spas and have your photo taken by a professional. Plus, receive $1,000 U.S. spending money!

Flowers...long walks...dinner for two... how does Silhouette Books make romance come alive for you?

Send us a script, with 500 words or less, along with visuals (only drawings, magazine cutouts or photographs or combination thereof). Show us how Silhouette Makes Your Love Come Alive. Be creative and have fun. No purchase necessary. All entries must be clearly marked with your name, address and telephone number. All entries will become property of Silhouette and are not returnable. **Contest closes September 28, 2001.**

Please send your entry to: **Silhouette Makes You a Star!**

In U.S.A.
P.O. Box 9069
Buffalo, NY, 14269-9069

In Canada
P.O. Box 637
Fort Erie, ON, L2A 5X3

Look for contest details on the next page, by visiting www.eHarlequin.com or request a copy by sending a self-addressed envelope to the applicable address above. Contest open to Canadian and U.S. residents who are 18 or over. Void where prohibited.

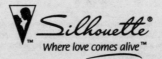

Silhouette®
Where love comes alive™

Our lucky winner's photo will appear in a Silhouette ad. Join the fun!

SRMYAS1

HARLEQUIN "SILHOUETTE MAKES YOU A STAR!" CONTEST 1308
OFFICIAL RULES
NO PURCHASE NECESSARY TO ENTER

1. To enter, follow directions published in the offer to which you are responding. Contest begins June 1, 2001, and ends on September 28, 2001. Entries must be postmarked by September 28, 2001, and received by October 5, 2001. Enter by hand-printing (or typing) on an 8 1/2" x 11" piece of paper your name, address (including zip code), contest number/name and attaching a script containing <u>500 words or less, along with drawings, photographs or magazine cutouts, or combinations thereof</u> (i.e., collage) <u>on no larger than 9" x 12"</u> piece of paper, describing how the <u>Silhouette books make romance come alive for you.</u> Mail via first-class mail to: Harlequin "Silhouette Makes You a Star!" Contest 1308, (in the U.S.) P.O. Box 9069, Buffalo, NY 14269-9069, (in Canada) P.O. Box 637, Fort Erie, Ontario, Canada L2A 5X3. Limit one entry per person, household or organization.

2. Contests will be judged by a panel of members of the Harlequin editorial, marketing and public relations staff. Fifty percent of criteria will be judged against script and fifty percent will be judged against drawing, photographs and/or magazine cutouts. Judging criteria will be based on the following:

   - Sincerity—25%
   - Originality and Creativity—50%
   - Emotionally Compelling—25%

   In the event of a tie, duplicate prizes will be awarded. Decisions of the judges are final.

3. All entries become the property of Torstar Corp. and may be used for future promotional purposes. Entries will not be returned. No responsibility is assumed for lost, late, illegible, incomplete, inaccurate, nondelivered or misdirected mail.

4. Contest open only to residents of the U.S. (<u>except Puerto Rico</u>) and Canada who are 18 years of age or older, and is void wherever prohibited by law; all applicable laws and regulations apply. Any litigation within the Province of Quebec respecting the conduct or organization of a publicity contest may be submitted to the Régie des alcools, des courses et des jeux for a ruling. Any litigation respecting the awarding of a prize may be submitted to the Régie des alcools, des courses et des jeux only for the purpose of helping the parties reach a settlement. Employees and immediate family members of Torstar Corp. and D. L. Blair, Inc., their affiliates, subsidiaries and all other agencies, entities and persons connected with the use, marketing or conduct of this contest are not eligible to enter. Taxes on prizes are the sole responsibility of the winner. Acceptance of any prize offered constitutes permission to use winner's name, photograph or other likeness for the purposes of advertising, trade and promotion on behalf of Torstar Corp., its affiliates and subsidiaries without further compensation to the winner, unless prohibited by law.

5. Winner will be determined no later than November 30, 2001, and will be notified by mail. Winner will be required to sign and return an Affidavit of Eligibility/Release of Liability/Publicity Release form within 15 days after winner notification. Noncompliance within that time period may result in disqualification and an alternative winner may be selected. All travelers must execute a Release of Liability prior to ticketing and must possess required travel documents (e.g., passport, photo ID) where applicable. Trip must be booked by December 31, 2001, and completed within one year of notification. No substitution of prize permitted by winner. Torstar Corp. and D. L. Blair, Inc., their parents, affiliates and subsidiaries are not responsible for errors in printing of contest, entries and/or game pieces. In the event of printing or other errors that may result in unintended prize values or duplication of prizes, all affected game pieces or entries shall be null and void. **Purchase or acceptance of a product offer does not improve your chances of winning.**

6. Prizes: (1) Grand Prize—A 2-night/3-day trip for two (2) to New York City, including round-trip coach air transportation nearest winner's home and hotel accommodations (double occupancy) at The Plaza Hotel, a glamorous afternoon makeover at <u>a trendy New York spa</u>, $1,000 in U.S. spending money and an opportunity to <u>have a professional photo taken and appear in a Silhouette advertisement</u> (approximate retail value: $7,000). (10) Ten Runner-Up Prizes of gift packages (retail value $50 ea.). Prizes consist of only those items listed as part of the prize. Limit one prize per person. Prize is valued in U.S. currency.

7. For the name of the winner (available after December 31, 2001) send a self-addressed, stamped envelope to: Harlequin "Silhouette Makes You a Star!" Contest 1197 Winners, P.O. Box 4200 Blair, NE 68009-4200 or you may access the www.eHarlequin.com Web site through February 28, 2002.

Contest sponsored by Torstar Corp., P.O Box 9042, Buffalo, NY 14269-9042.

SRMYAS2

COMING NEXT MONTH

#1381 HARD TO FORGET—Annette Broadrick
Man of the Month
Although Joe Sanchez hadn't seen Elena Moldonado in over ten years, he'd never forgotten his high school sweetheart. Now that Elena was back in town, Joe wanted her back in *his* arms. The stormy passion between them proved as wild as ever, but Joe would have to regain Elena's trust before he'd have a chance at the love of a lifetime.

#1382 A LOVING MAN—Cait London
Rose Granger didn't want to have a thing to do with worldly and sophisticated Stefan Donatien! She preferred her life just as it was, without the risk of heartbreak. Besides, what could the handsome Stefan possibly see in a simple small-town woman? But Stefan's tender seductions were irresistible, and Rose found herself wishing he would stay…forever.

#1383 HAVING HIS CHILD—Amy J. Fetzer
Wife, Inc./The Baby Bank
With no husband in sight and her biological clock ticking, Angela Justice figured the local sperm bank was the only way to make her dreams of having a baby come true. That was before Angela's best friend, Dr. Lucas Ryder, discovered her plans and decided to grant her wish—the old-fashioned way!

#1384 BABY OF FORTUNE—Shirley Rogers
Fortunes of Texas: The Lost Heirs
Upon discovering that he was an heir to the famed Fortune clan, Justin Bond resolved to give his marriage a second chance. His estranged wife, Heather, was more than willing to welcome Justin back into her life. But would Justin welcome Heather back into his heart when he learned the secret his wife had kept from him?

#1385 UNDERCOVER SULTAN—Alexandra Sellers
Sons of the Desert: The Sultans
When corporate spy Mariel de Vouvray was forced into an uneasy partnership with Sheikh Haroun al Jawadi, her powerful attraction to him didn't make things any easier! With every new adventure, Mariel fell further under the spell of her seductive sheikh, and soon she longed to make their partnership into something far more permanent.

#1386 BEAUTY IN HIS BEDROOM—Ashley Summers
Clint Whitfield came home after two years overseas and found feisty Regina Flynn living in his mansion. His first instinct was to throw the lovely strawberry blond intruder off his property—and out of his life. His second instinct was to let her stay—and to persuade the delectable Gina *into* his bedroom!

SDCNM0701